The Gatekeeper

The Gatekeep

Ian Taylor, Rosi Tayl

Chapter One

Low Moor was a village of forty semi-detached rented cottages, that formed the shape of a vesica piscis around the village green. The cottages were inhabited entirely by local families, none of whom had ever left, but had handed their tenancies down through succeeding generations for as long as anyone could remember. Their landlord was the Church of England and the rents were comparatively low, as a result it was a community where change was minimal.

All the cottages in the village had large gardens, where tenants grew vegetables and fruit and kept livestock. The largest garden to the eastern end of the village green was the walled garden that belonged to the vicarage. Its neatly trimmed lawn was surrounded by mature native trees – mostly oak and birch – and flowering shrubs. A flight of stone steps led up from the front lawn to a paved terrace, bordered by shapely stone balusters supporting a balustrade of the same stone and ornamental urns. The impression was not one of opulence, but of considerable status and aspiring gentility.

Beyond the terrace the three-storey gritstone Victorian vicarage was dark and silent under its heavy slab roof. In contrast with the tidy garden the house had the appearance of a place recently abandoned, an impression suggested by a broken first-floor window and sagging curtains detached from their runners. The massive oaken front door beneath its columned portico was deepy scarred by time and uncontrolled ivy rioted over the facade and dangled from the guttering in tangled clumps. Its visual appearance added to the building's atmosphere of neglect and incipient decay.

A small stone-built cottage sat in the south-east corner of the garden, bordered on the two inward-facing sides by low box hedges and rose bushes. On the eastern side of the vicarage was a well stocked kitchen garden. To the rear was a cobbled yard with old stone ranges, mostly used in the past for stabling. On the west was a short gravelled drive leading from an imposing gritstone-pillared gateway with tall wrought-iron gates.

It was a vicarage typical of its period: large, austere and a little forbidding.

A tall dog-collared figure, dressed entirely in black, including an old-fashioned preacher-style hat, strode up the drive from the wrought-iron entrance gates. The figure carried an ebony staff held tightly against his right shoulder. A sunwheel symbol showing the cardinal points and the cross-quarters occupied the crook at the head of the staff.

At sixty years of age Reverend Julius Dodds was a man who projected an air of absolute authority. His height of six feet five inches was intimidating enough. Add a sleek mane of steel-grey hair, eyes of the coldest blue that rarely blinked and a voice whose power and resonance could fill a cathedral, you had a man accustomed to getting his own way. Even the bishop felt reduced in his presence. Julius Dodds was a man who brushed obstacles aside like a gardener might waft away summer flies.

Four monks, young, blond and oddly expressionless, clad in dark brown habits, followed Dodds to the vicarage door. They stood behind him as he thundered on the door with his staff, as if he meant to shatter the time-worn oak to splinters.

"Reverend Oliver," Dodds boomed, "you must answer the door! If you do not, we will enter the house!"

Michael Oliver, the forty-year-old vicar, wild-haired, unshaven and unwashed, was too preoccupied to pay attention to Dodds's summons. He was chasing Olwen Williams, a local beauty from the nearby village of Walden, around his bedroom in his underwear. It was a ritual they indulged in most days.

"Oh, Olwen, you are so unkind," the vicar cried, "let me touch your gorgeous breasts, just for a moment, you know how they excite me!"

Olwen laughed and threw off her clothes. "You must do something for me first, my handsome priest. Down on your knees!"

The vicar obeyed. "Oh, Olwen, let me drink from your endless fountain of life!"

She grasped his hair and pressed his head between her legs. "Drink, priest! And be reborn!"

Moments later they flung themselves on to the bed in a wild embrace…

Dodds continued to hammer on the battered door. "I'm asking you again, Reverend Oliver. Come to the door or we will open it ourselves!"

In the bedroom Olwen and the vicar, sweating heavily, rolled apart.

"Knock, knock! Who's there i' the name of Beelzebub?" The vicar laughed, quoting the Porter from *Macbeth.*

The thundering on the door came again.

"Knock, knock! Who's there, in the other devil's name?"

"Don't you want to know who it is?" Olwen asked, running her fingers along the vicar's thighs. "It might be important."

The vicar gazed at her like a lovesick adolescent. "Nothing's more important than this. Being here with you. You're my life, you know you are."

Dodds pounded on the door.

"Knock, knock! This is hell-gate indeed!" The vicar rolled off the bed. "I'll get rid of them and be right back." He pulled on his shirt and pants and hurried from the room.

When he had gone Olwen morphed from her seductress to her maternal archetype and left the room. Her long-term lover Gareth met her on the landing.

"It's Dodds," he said.

"I know. Let's watch from the garden."

They hurried down the back stairs and out into the yard.

The churchwardens of Low Moor benefice, a couple in their mid-sixties, appeared from the corner cottage: Arthur Hall, wiry and weather-beaten and his wife Beryl, stocky and strong.

They looked troubled as they hurried across the lawn towards Dodds and his monks by the vicarage door.

"Whatever's going on?" Beryl queried anxiously.

"Is there a problem, Reverend Dodds?" Arthur asked.

Dodds glared at them coldly. Arthur and Beryl looked down, intimidated.

"The spare key, if you please," Dodds demanded.

Without a word Arthur handed over a large iron key. At a sign from Dodds a monk ushered them back towards their cottage.

"Return to your house," the monk intoned flatly, but firmly. "There's nothing to concern you here."

Arthur and Beryl turned unhappily away. They stood in the cottage doorway, watching apprehensively, as Dodds inserted the key and unlocked the vicarage door. The four monks followed him into the house.

A wide oak-panelled staircase led off the stone-flagged entrance hall. The walls of the staircase and the landing above were hung with paintings: a dozen dark moorland scenes filled with strange swirling energy, slightly reminiscent of the work of Edvard Munch. Sinister anthropomorphic rocks occupied the foreground. Dodds scowled at the paintings with obvious repugnance.

Michael Oliver appeared on the landing. He glared at Dodds and his monks in outrage.

"How dare you come in here? Out of my house, Julius Dodds – and take your brown thugs with you!"

Dodds ignored the vicar's words. He turned to the monks. "Take him!"

The four monks sprang up the stairs and grabbed the vicar, forcing him to the floor.

"You can't do this! You have no authority!" the vicar cried in furious dismay.

Dodds's glance of icy wrath reduced him to silence. "You're a disgrace to the cloth, Reverend Oliver! The bishop has requested your removal. Bring him down!"

The monks frogmarched the vicar down the stairs. Their captive struggled vainly to free himself. "No! No! Let me go!"

Dodds ignored the vicar's cries. The monks brought the wretched man down to the entrance hall and stood him before Dodds. Even the outraged vicar was unable to meet the man's domineering gaze.

"You have made a mockery of your vocation. You have allowed *that witch* to defile this sacred institution. I am officially removing you from office.Take him away!" Dodds added as an afterthought: "Two of you stay and get rid of those vile paintings."

Two monks dragged Michael Oliver to the door. The others started removing the paintings from the landing walls. Dodds looked on in grim satisfaction, then turned on his heel and left the house.

The two monks propelled their captive down the drive towards the wrought-iron gates and a waiting Mercedes Panel Van. They paid no attention to the ex-vicar's cries. Dodds followed them, deep in his thoughts.

A slight movement among the garden bushes revealed Olwen, with her long dark hair and sallow complexion, watching triumphantly as Michael Oliver, weeping now, was led away…

One of the monks made a bonfire at the northern end of the kitchen garden next to the wall of the old stable block. He prepared a solid base of kindling, on to which he threw the paintings one at a time. His companion carried more paintings from the house and placed them ready to be cast on the fire.

Meanwhile, in the yard at the back of the vicarage, Olwen and her companions, the sultry Rhiannon, dark-haired Gareth, fair-complexioned Rhys and Gwenda with her head of auburn curls, assembled new paintings and carried them into the house through the back door. The paintings revealed similar moorland scenes, with sinister anthropomorphic rocks in the foreground. Olwen and her friends laughed, darkly amused.

They leaned the paintings against the wall in an empty attic at the eastern end of the house and covered them with a dust sheet. They looked from the gable-end window, which had a view of the two monks tending their fire in the kitchen garden.

"We've lost a vicar," Gwenda said with feigned regret. "The poor man was weeping for the joys he left behind."

"We'll soon get another," Rhys commented. "Dodds makes John Knox look like a pussy. He'll never give up."

"Let's hope the next vicar will be as obliging as dear old Olly!" Rhiannon's comment had them all laughing, but their light-hearted banter was belied by the expression of dark purpose in their eyes.

"What fun!" Gareth announced, looking down at the monks. "Dodds has left us a little game to play."

"I'll bet his cyborgs can't afford life insurance!" Rhiannon laughed.

Opening the window, they took deep breaths and blew hard towards the fire. The monks choked with the sudden billowing clouds of bonfire smoke and clutched their throats. The fire leaped at them like a living being, clinging to them like napalm. The monks' habits quickly began to burn.

Olwen and her companions continued to blow from the open window.

Arthur and Beryl, clutching blankets, ran from their cottage towards the fire. They tried to smother the burning monks, who writhed and cried out in increasing agony.

"Quick, Beryl! Fetch more blankets!" Arthur urged in desperation.

"Oh, God help us!" Beryl ran back in panic to the cottage.

No matter how many blankets Beryl brought the fire devoured them in a matter of seconds. It was as if the flames were possessed by a ferocious spirit that was impossible to subdue. The heat became too intense for the churchwardens to bear.

"Get back!" Arthur yelled. "It's no good!"

Arthur and Beryl moved away from the fire, clinging to each other in terror.

The fire consumed the monks. They screamed and collapsed to the ground, reduced to charred residues, like victims of a rocket attack.

The sound of Olwen's laughter wafted across the garden in the wind.

Chapter Two

In a spacious well-appointed room in the bishop's palace Julius Dodds took tea with Hugh Mortimer, the bishop, a man of slightly younger age with short greying hair, whose sensitive features bore signs of irritation. The two men sipped tea from rose-patterned porcelain tea cups. Neither spoke for some time. Dodds frowned slightly, brooding. The bishop watched him with a hint of impatience.

"The parishes of Low Moor and Walden, My Lord Bishop." Dodds began at last in a formal tone heavy with protracted reflection.

The bishop winced. He disliked formalities and had no intention of employing them now. He realised they were Dodds's way of keeping him at a distance. "Indeed. Such troublesome parishes, Julius. We must find a permanent solution."

Dodds studied his large hands. He liked to keep this particular bishop waiting. Formalities had been abandoned early, he noted, so there was nothing to be gained from using them further. Eventually he sat back in his chair and met the bishop's gaze. "Well, Hugh, you will be pleased to know I've a new vicar in mind for them."

The bishop glanced away. He hated those ice-cold eyes. Though he had only held his office for two years he had grown to dislike everything about Julius Dodds, the exact opposite of his predecessor, who had nothing but praise for the man. He found Dodds arrogant and secretive, with a manner distantly reminiscent of the Inquisition's fanatics.

Where did he recruit his brown-robed monks? What was their purpose? Who did he really work for? He had tried many times to probe without result. Julius Dodds was as impenetrable as a wall of gritstone rock.

The bishop raised an enquiring eyebrow. "Have you now? You're certain he has the right qualities? Can he draw those recalcitrant locals back into the fold?"

Dodds studied the bishop with his unblinking gaze. "He's strong-minded. Devout. Pure in spirit."

The bishop doubted that Dodds was the best judge of spiritual qualities. But, provisionally at any rate, he had to accept the man's assessment. It would soon become clear if he was right.

"Well let us hope he remains so, Julius." He added as an afterthought. "On all three counts."

"I have confidence in him." Dodds knew the bishop wouldn't wish for any direct involvement in the appointment of a new incumbent to these particular parishes. Past bishops had always left such difficult matters to the Church's troubleshooter. Dodds wondered, with growing impatience, how many platitudes he would have to endure before he could get back to his work. As far as he was concerned the business was sorted.

"We must pray the new man will cope better than Reverend Oliver. And all the poor souls that laboured in vain before him. We have lost so many good men in those parishes. It's time we found an incumbent with the sense of mission to solve the problem."

"This one has a wife."

"Ah, moral support. That's good." The bishop offered a hopeful smile, but privately he wondered if any wife would last long in such a challenging environment. "With God's grace –"

Dodds cut him off. "Yes... well, Hugh, I felt you'd want to be informed as a matter of priority."

The bishop bristled. The man was impossible! "Indeed, Julius, I consider it your duty to tell me everything you consider to be relevant with regard to fresh appointments to those parishes."

Dodds shot the bishop a disdainful glance. He did not condescend to reply.

The bishop felt irritated again. How dare the man force him to ask? "Their names, Julius, if you'd be so kind. I'll pray for them."

"Paul and Sarah Milton," Dodds replied. "They've been working most successfully in South London."

"Low Moor and Walden will be rather a culture shock, don't you think?"

"I have chosen the right man," Dodds said coldly. "I'm certain he will prevail."

* * *

Shabby blocks of flats and boarded-up shops lined both sides of the street. A church and church hall stood mid-way down. A few cars swished past in the unrelenting rain. Half a dozen pedestrians hurried towards the hall.

The interior of the hall, though drab, was warm and brightly lit. Paul Milton, the thirty-year-old vicar, boyishly good-looking under his mop of brown curls, stood on a dais with his wife Sarah, a delicate English Rose.

John, a young black vicar, waited to one side, watching Andy, the churchwarden, as he briefly took the floor.

"Friends – we're here to say a sad farewell to our beloved vicar, Reverend Paul and to his dear wife, Sarah. The church has come back to life since they joined us. Thanks to them we're a real community again. Everyone has found a welcoming home here, no matter their cultural origins or the colour of their skin. We are a family of equals, with no-one more equal than anyone else!"

The mixed gathering of sixty poor people cheered and clapped.

"We certainly are!" shouted an earnest middle-aged white woman.

"Thank the Lord for Reverend Paul!" an ebullient black woman yelled.

"We'll miss you both," Andy continued, "but we wish you well with your new challenge."

Paul raised his hands to quieten the ripple of applause. "You're wonderful people! We'll never forget our three years here. We hope we've made a difference to your lives, as you've certainly made to ours."

"Yeah, man! Yeah! We love you, man!" an enthusiastic black youth called out.

The room was filled with prolonged applause.

Paul signalled to the young black vicar, who stepped forward to stand at his side. "I'd like to introduce Reverend John, who'll be carrying on the work. Please give him your wholehearted support."

Everyone in the room clapped and cheered. Sarah sat at the piano.

"Gonna be a hard act to follow." Reverend John beamed at his new congregation. "But, with God's help – and yours – we'll do it. Together!"

The room filled with shouts of *Yeah! We're with you, man! Together!*

Sarah played a modern hymn. Paul and John led the congregation in the singing.

* * *

Paul's aging Ford Fiesta, its back seat filled with boxes and cases, headed up the motorway among heavy traffic. Signs appeared for *The North, York, Leeds.* Paul, dressed in clerical collar and dark suit, was behind the wheel. Sarah, in a smart pastel suit, looked up from a road map.

"So we've no congregation in the church at Low Moor? Is the village all holiday lets?"

"Not at all. Reverend Dodds said all the houses are lived in by locals." He pulled a puzzled face. "But, in spite of that, we've apparently not even one worshipper. Rev D said the previous vicar, Michael Oliver, became ill and wasn't able to fulfil his duties. I got the impression his congregation just drifted away."

"What was wrong with the poor vicar?"

"Rev D didn't go into details. He just said the locals had become more interested in tending their gardens than attending church."

"So they need to be re-enthused."

"Nice word! Yes, they need reawakening."

"Well, what could be harder than our achievement in London? Both the church and church hall were closed when we arrived."

"I can't imagine anything tougher than that. But this will be a very different sort of place." He fell silent, studying his mirror as he pulled out to overtake a slow-moving truck. "I just can't understand why Rev D didn't offer us another urban parish. After all, that's our background."

"Perhaps this appointment is in way of a thank you for the last three years' hard work, with no more than a dozen days off to visit our families."

"Rev D didn't strike me as a man who was into thank yous. But you'd think there'd be other vicars more suitable, who've had years of experience of country life."

"Are you starting to have doubts?"

"No...not really. I just can't figure out Rev D's thinking. I'll need a completely different skillset from London – no happy clappy services up here! A much more sober approach will be the best way forward."

"I'm certain you'll manage that! And I'll be there to help you."

"Sure you won't be lonely, stuck out in the wilds?"

She laughed. "I'll be busy – with a full-time job supporting my wonderful husband!"

"I'm so glad I've got you," he gave her a radiant smile. "We'll have them back in church within six months!"

They turned off the motorway and entered immediately into steeper terrain. Craggy cliffs reared ahead of them, topped with wild fringes of wind-blasted trees. An occasional waterfall cascaded over the edge, gleaming like jewels in the sunlight.

"You know, this could be our chance to start a family." Sarah smiled brightly at the passing fields and woodland. "We've been married almost four years. People in London were asking if we were planning to."

"God willing," Paul replied a little stiffly. "After all, it's our sacred duty."

"I don't want God in bed with me, Paul – I want you!" she countered testily.

There was a moment of tension between them.

"I think we should get used to our new parishes before we decide about that," he stated firmly.

She continued as if he hadn't spoken. "Village life will be so much healthier for little ones, won't it?"

"And for you as well," he replied with a glance of concern. "That's one of the reasons I took the appointment."

"I'm better now," she insisted. "You know I am. I've got over mum's death completely. But thanks anyway for thinking of me."

He looked at her doubtfully, but chose not to disagree. Her highly-strung temperament had become much more brittle in the twelve months since her mother died. He didn't want an argument – that would be a bad beginning for what he hoped would be an invigorating rural appointment.

The Fiesta moved slowly between farm fields and woods as it gradually climbed, on narrowing roads, into a rugged landscape of steep drystone-walled fields and blocks of rocky woodland. As they drove over the brow of a hill the view suddenly opened up.

"Just look at that!" she exclaimed.

Ahead of them high moorland skylines stretched into the far distance. On the lower slopes the heather had come into bloom, forming a bright purple expanse. He pulled into a lay-by so they could take it in.

They sat for a while in absorbed silence.

"How could anyone have problems with views like this on the doorstep?" she wondered aloud. "Surely they uplift the spirit?"

"Perhaps some unfortunate folk have very little spirit left in them to be uplifted by anything," he mused. "Bad health and disappointment can affect anyone anywhere."

"But we shouldn't have that kind of problem in Low Moor. These are issues we've left behind."

"But we still mustn't be complacent. The locals might be harder to win back than we think. They might have grown used to a life without

God. They may think they can lead fulfilling lives without Him. But that's impossible. No-one can lead a meaningful life without God. I must lead these people by example."

"Just don't get too fanatical," she warned. "People need love too."

* * *

They drove deeper into the moors, following winding lanes above which the heather-clad slopes stretched away. After another half hour's driving they entered a steep-sided valley and almost at once came upon the village sign *LOW MOOR* by the side of the road. The sign was surrounded by a border of summer flowers.

Semi-detached stone-built cottages stood back from the village green, through which a brisk stream flowed, spanned by several small bridges. It seemed picture postcard perfect.

Villagers of all ages worked in their gardens, tending the fruit and flowers. They stared suspiciously as Paul and Sarah drove past. Paul waved and smiled at the people closest to the road. But, though they couldn't fail to see him, they wasn't a single friendly acknowledgement.

"Stunning reception!" He pulled a face. "Have to get a labrador and green wellies, then maybe they'll speak to me!"

"You'll win them back." Sarah waved and smiled at the unresponsive villagers. "You're the best God salesman I know!"

They laughed.

"Look," she exclaimed, "there's our church!"

They glimpsed a squat Norman tower, built from the local gritstone, through the leaves of encircling oaks, which grew just inside the surrounding wall of the extensive churchyard.

"And there's our house. My goodness, it's huge!"

Since Reverend Oliver had departed the vicarage had been smartened up. The broken window had been repaired and the sagging curtains re-hung. The ivy had been trimmed back and the scarred front door repainted. Lights were on in the ground-floor rooms. The impression of abandonment and decay appeared to have been driven out like unwanted squatters.

The wrought-iron gates were wide open, so they pulled on to the short gravel drive. Arthur and Beryl Hall, dressed smartly, stood by the columned portico. Reverend Dodds, in his black hat, waited with suppressed impatience a little apart from them.

Paul and Sarah climbed from the car. Dodds shook hands with them.

"I'm pleased to see you, Reverend Milton." He cast an approving eye over Sarah. "And your charming wife." He turned towards Arthur and Beryl. "These are your churchwardens. Also gardeners, cooks and general maintenance people. Their assistance will allow you time to focus on your work."

Arthur and Beryl introduced themselves and shook hands with Paul and Sarah. Paul noticed the Halls seemed uneasy in the presence of Reverend Dodds.

Arthur pointed to his cottage. "We're just there, whenever you need us, Reverend Milton."

"Why don't you make yourself at home, Sarah?" Beryl asked. "You'll be weary. I'll put the kettle on."

Sarah, Beryl and Arthur went into the vicarage. Reverend Dodds handed Paul a large bunch of keys. He glanced towards the church and churchyard beyond the south wall of the vicarage garden.

"The keys for All Saints church. Never leave it unlocked."

"Thieves, Reverend Dodds? Out here?" Paul asked in surprise.

"We have our share of... undesirables." Dodds replied without elaboration."You'll come across them."

Paul met Dodds's gaze. "Why choose me for this place? I'm an urban person. The closest I've got to the countryside is my parents' garden in Oxford!"

Reverend Dodds was used to people treating him with deference, but this young man was a rare exception. His new incumbent faced him forcefully and did not flinch from his gaze. "I understood you relished a challenge?" he said at last. "Well, you'll have one here."

"Do you have the keys for the church in my other parish?" Paul asked.

"St Martin's church in the parish of Walden is a ruin. You won't need any keys for that."

"So the parish of Walden has no active church and no population?"

"There's a community of sorts up there," Dodds stated disparagingly. "You'll meet them."

He turned away and set off walking towards the wrought-iron gates. Paul hurried after him.

"Can you tell me more about the sort of challenge we face here? I think it's important to prepare myself. Don't you?"

Reverend Dodds had reached the main gates. He turned to Paul. "In London you encouraged the willing poor to form a Christian community. Those who wished became part of it. Here you must expect active opposition. I'm sure you will deal with it appropriately. I'm here to advise you, of course. We'll speak again soon." He touched his hat and walked away.

"What do you mean by active opposition?" Paul shouted at Dodds's back.

But Reverend Dodds got into his brand new SUV and drove away without another word.

Chapter Three

After Beryl had left them Paul and Sarah sat at opposite ends of the large oak table in the cavernous vicarage kitchen eating slices of Beryl's sponge cake and drinking tea.

She put her plate aside. "Just imagine, in years gone by this table would have been filled with the vicar's children. I would think you could get at least ten more people round here!"

She noticed the sudden tension in his shoulders and arms. She laughed. "There'd be a ready-made congregation – plus the servants, of course." She watched him relax.

"Everyone was expected to attend church back then," he said. "Parson Grimshaw of Haworth even chased them there with a whip! I can't imagine him putting up with *active opposition*!"

"Didn't Rev D say what the opposition was?" she asked.

"Lapsed Christians, I presume." He shrugged. "Who else?"

She looked mystified. "What are they opposing us with? And why?"

"It seems the good reverend is letting us find out for ourselves."

"That's unfair. We've only just arrived. We've no-one to ask."

"I'll speak to Arthur in the morning. He might be able to enlighten us."

"Well, if it's lapsed Christians we've won them back before."

"We must be positive. Let God fill our minds. There's no other guide."

"I try. Every day." Her face puckered with self doubt. "But my faith's not as strong as yours."

"But it's *there*." He looked at her earnestly. "You can build on that."

She turned away and stood up to pour more tea, then emitted a little cry of surprise. Olwen Williams in her maternal aspect was staring at them through the window.

"Aha!" he exclaimed. "A lapsed Christian!"

He opened the back door with what he felt was an appropriate flourish. Olwen stood on the doorstep.

She smiled at him. "Did I startle you? I'm Olwen Williams. I live up the road – in Walden."

"Paul Milton."

They shook hands. He was surprised by the strength of her grip.

"I saw the car...I thought Reverend Oliver had come back. We were great friends, he and I."

"I'm afraid he's ill and won't be resuming his duties. I'm his replacement."

She gave him a strong penetrating look. He shifted uneasily, but held her gaze. What was it with these people, he wondered, who tried to stare through you? Dodds was bad enough. But this Olwen woman was even worse! To his relief Sarah joined him at the door.

"This is my wife, Sarah. Sarah, meet Olwen Williams from Walden."

"Hi, Olwen. Pleased to meet you." Sarah smiled innocently at Olwen.

Normally he would have invited her into the house, but for some unclear reason was reluctant to do so. There was something about this woman that made him feel uncomfortable. He wondered if Sarah had picked up a similar vibe.

"Have you come far?" Olwen asked.

"From London." Sarah laughed. "It seems like we've arrived in a whole other world!"

Olwen gazed searchingly at Sarah, who seemed unable to take her eyes off her.

"You look like a real country girl to me." Olwen smiled, tilting her head provocatively to one side.

"I'll do my best to be one," Sarah replied demurely.

Olwen shifted her attention to Paul, her eyes playing boldly over his features. "I hope you find your true destiny here, Reverend Milton."

Paul felt confused. Olwen's formal platitude was entirely at odds with the undeniably invasive way she was looking at him.

He continued to hold her gaze. "I've found it already, but thanks anyway."

Olwen seemed suddenly to tire of the conversation, as if she had seen enough of the new incumbent to form a convincing appraisal of him. She turned to go. "My regards to Reverend Oliver if you should see him."

Sarah went back into the house as Paul, seized by a sudden afterthought, shouted after Olwen.

"Come to church! This Sunday! Bring your friends!"

Olwen morphed spontaneously into her younger seductress form, a twenty-year-old raven-haired beauty. She turned and smiled at Paul suggestively. He stared at her, startled. Just as suddenly she returned to her older self, crossed the cobbled stableyard and disappeared through a door in the wall that led into the lane to Walden.

* * *

Paul and Sarah climbed the vicarage stairs. There were no paintings on either the staircase or the landing.

"What do you think, Sarah?" he asked. "Didn't that Olwen Williams strike you as a bit strange?"

"Not at all." She frowned at him. "She seemed very kind. Quite motherly."

"I thought she was odd," he stated emphatically, thinking of Olwen's uncompromising stare.

"Well I didn't! I thought she was charming."

As so often these days, he realised sadly, she didn't seem to value his opinions, preferring her own point of view, which was, increasingly, beyond debate.

She stood on the landing, which ran the length of the house, looking at a row of closed doors. "Beryl said she'd given us the master bedroom and made up the bed for us. But which room is it?"

"Better take a look. I think there are supposed to be at least four bedrooms on this floor."

They opened doors and peered into rooms. They quickly found the right one. It was a large room with a four-poster bed, which stood in imposing isolation half way along an interior wall. Arthur had placed their belongings beneath the window opposite.

"Oh, fantastic!" she exclaimed. "Always wanted a four-poster! Think of the times we'll have in this!"

"Making babies!" he laughed.

"And having fun!" she added with a mischievous glance.

She leaped on to the bed and closed the heavy curtains. "Oh, who can help me? Am I lost in this darkness for ever?"

To his surprise he found himself caught up by her sudden high spirits. "Fair damsel, do not fear! The hero is speeding to your rescue!"

He flung off his jacket, parted the curtains and dived in to join her. They rolled together on the bed and kissed with growing passion. He fondled her breasts. She began to undo his trousers. Suddenly he froze.

"Maybe we shouldn't do this."

"You're right," she agreed. "Let's get undressed or we'll ruin our best clothes."

He eased himself away from her and stood up. "That's not what I meant. Work first. We should save this for later."

"Can I look forward to it?" she asked hopefully.

He gave her a non-committal smile. She turned away, trying to hide her disappointment.

They explored the attics, five large rooms which corresponded with the four bedrooms below, plus one attic room above the smaller study and bathroom. The rooms were full of stored items: bed frames, trunks, old-fashioned wash stands, rolled carpets, standard lamps and paintings covered with a dust sheet. Sarah prowled through the rooms, fascinated by everything.

He looked from a back attic window. Beyond the vicarage yard a vast expanse of purple heather stretched away towards darker, more remote moorland horizons. In the middle distance the scattered cottages of Walden nestled among the deep woods that fringed the foot of the heather-clad slopes. In the foreground were a couple of field barns belonging to Low Moor.

"Sarah!" he called. "You can see Walden. I've a ruined church somewhere up there. St Martin's. Right out of a gothic novel!"

She called from an adjacent room. "Paul...look at this!"

He realised she had chosen to ignore his excited outburst. He wondered what she could have found in these musty old rooms that was in any way intriguing. He saw she had removed the dust cover from a row of paintings and had arranged some of them to face the room. The brooding moorland scenes with their strange swirling energy, twisted trees and dark jumbled rocks filled him with revulsion.

"I've never seen anything like them," she enthused. "So powerful. Such assured brushwork."

"I think they're hideous!" he stated decisively.

She looked closely at the signature. "They're hers! Olwen Williams'! I'd like to put one up."

"Not in this vicarage!" he growled.

She looked hurt. He immediately regretted his outburst.

"Okay," he conceded. "One. And put it somewhere discreet."

They left the attics and descended to the dining room, where Beryl had left them an appropriate summer evening meal of salad and cold meat. They ate hungrily, in silence. Eventually Sarah stood up.

"I'm tired. I'm going up. Will you be long?"

"Just a few minutes."

He watched her leave the room, then took his prayer book and read aloud:

"*We pray for the spiritual needs of the villages in our land...*

The words scrambled on the page. New words replaced them:

I WANT TO MAKE LOVE EACH TIME I THINK OF YOU

He stood up in dismay and stared at the prayer book. The words scrambled again:

WHAT DO YOU WANT PRIEST WHEN YOU THINK OF ME?

He dropped the book as if it had burst into flames. He sat abruptly at the table, sweating with shock. What was happening? Was he becoming ill?

Olwen's soft laughter rippled like a gentle breeze through the room.

* * *

Deep in the woods of Walden Olwen was at work in the basement of her ancient cottage. The room's detail was hidden in shadow, lit only by a small peat fire and a single candle that stood in a carved ram's horn holder in the centre of the plain oak table.

Olwen was alone, bent over a black scrying mirror, which lay tilted slightly toward her at one end of the table. In the mirror Paul's distraught face could be seen.

She stood up and threw a cloth, heavily embroidered with mystical symbols, over the mirror and moved to a rocking chair by the fire. She laughed quietly as she rocked herself backwards and forwards.

* * *

Sarah slept peacefully in the four-poster bed. Paul thrashed around, as though struggling with an invisible assailant. He woke suddenly, as if a sound had disturbed him. He sat up in bed, listening. A whisper, very faint, seemed to come to him from the direction of the window:

Paul... can you hear me? Come to me now... come to me now... come to me now...

He hesitated a moment, then went to the window and looked out. The moon raced through ragged clumps of cumulus. Out on the moors a line of lights threaded its way through the darkness.

A group of cloaked and hooded figures, carrying lanterns, made its way in single file across the moor. One of the figures, its features hidden within its hood, turned around and cast a white silk scarf into the air...

Paul peered from the bedroom window. A bird, with the plumage of a barn owl, appeared in the moonlight and hovered outside the glass. The bird had Paul's face. The face addressed him through the window in an eerie electronic voice:

God doesn't exist, you deluded idiot! Your belief is a lie! There's nothing THERE!! A hole in the godless SKY!!

Paul's owl-face broke into metallic laughter.

He whipped the curtains closed in dismay and terror. What buried self-doubt was rearing up from its hidden tomb? After a few moments he parted the curtains and saw with relief that the bird had vanished.

Then he noticed a white silk scarf lying crumpled on the outside windowsill. He opened the window, retrieved the scarf and examined it. The scarf was plain, unadorned, with no identifying marks. He folded it carefully and placed it on the dressing table. He shook his head wonderingly. Too much coffee! he thought.

He climbed into bed and lay lost in his thoughts.

The next morning Sarah seemed still to be sleeping soundly. Paul woke and crossed to the dressing table. The white silk scarf had gone.

Chapter Four

The pre-Reformation church of All Saints stood in its churchyard surrounded by gravestones and encircling oaks. Paul and Sarah walked up the churchyard path from the private gate set in the south-west corner of their garden wall.

He studied the exterior of the building with absorbed concentration. "Late twelfth century. Early English. Simplicity and elegance." He beamed at the building with undisguised pleasure.

"Maybe, with all these oak trees, it was once a Druids' sacred grove." She laughed, to show that she wasn't being serious.

"What matters is that it's Christian now," he replied curtly.

They looked up at the corbel table, where a row of carved figures – gryphons, basilisks and bulging-eyed demons – glared down at them.

"Quite a gathering!" He laughed. "The mediaeval imagination was amazing!"

They unlocked the church door and went inside. He immediately climbed the steps to the pulpit, while she sat at the organ.

"There's an odd atmosphere in here, don't you think so, Paul?" she asked, pulling a face. "Very oppressive."

"It's just dead air," he said dismissively. "The place has been locked up so long. Good acoustics though. We'll have to choose some rousing hymns for the first service."

She played a few bars. "Fantastic tone! I'm going to love this!"

As the notes of the organ died away sounds could be heard, like the flapping of wings and the scrabbling of claws, high up in the shadowy corners of the dark pine-pannelled ceiling.

"Pigeons!" he exclaimed. "They get in everywhere!"

Arthur, in his work clothes, stepped into the nave. He had removed his cap and stuffed it into a pocket of his weather-faded outdoors' jacket. He seemed a little awkward. "I just heard the organ," he explained. "It's been quite a while since it was touched. Reverend Oliver got so he couldn't stand it."

Paul descended from the pulpit. "You're welcome, Arthur. I've a few questions to ask you, if you don't mind."

As Sarah played the hymn *Oh God, Our Help In Ages Past* softly in the background, the two men sat together in a pew.

"Who needs God when they think they live in an earthly paradise? What would you say to that, Arthur?" Paul smiled encouragingly at the churchwarden.

"If you're talking about the lack of a congregation it's not quite as simple as that, Reverend Milton," Arthur replied in his strong northern accent. "They don't come to church because they don't want to. They've turned away from it, deliberate like."

"I've been told to expect *active opposition.* Who's it going to come from?"

"Whatever's happened here it started way back in Walden," Arthur began after a lengthy silence. "There's never been much Christian faith in Walden. Low Moor's gone the same way. Oh, they dig their gardens. Keep the place tidy. They seem to enjoy their lives. But the church don't exist for 'em."

"Materialists." Paul shrugged. "Isn't it the same in most of village England?"

"It's not that." Arthur replied slowly, as if he was choosing his words with great care. "There are no yuppies here. There's something else at work."

Paul looked puzzled. "I don't follow you."

"It's in the air, like a fine summer rain. It soaks into you." Arthur studied the young vicar, as though trying to divine his powers of comprehension. "It's the influence from Walden. But it's beyond any man to prove it."

"What influence is this?" Paul asked with rising concern.

"You'll find out for yourself soon enough," Arthur stated darkly.

"What happened to my predecessor?"

"Reverend Oliver took ill...in the vicarage. Dodds closed the place up."

Paul noticed that Arthur pronounced the name Dodds with a downwards movement of his lips, as if he had tasted food that was far from his liking.

"You're saying Michael Oliver had some kind of nervous breakdown?"

"You could put it like that," Arthur replied. "But you must decide for yourself." He got to his feet. "If you'll excuse me, Reverend Milton, I've work to do in the garden while the weather's fine."

Arthur walked from the church, leaving Paul deep in thought. Sarah stopped playing the hymn.

"What was all that about?"

"I don't honestly know," he said with a shrug.

* * *

Paul parked the Fiesta in the car park of St Stephen's Nursing Home. He took a small suitcase from the car and walked to the main entrance.

He approached the desk. The bright young receptionist greeted him with a practised smile.

"Paul Milton. I've some things for Michael Oliver." He indicated the suitcase.

"Oh, right. I remember you phoning. I'll get Darren to take you to him."

Minutes later Paul and Darren, a tall young male nurse, walked along a ground-floor corridor towards the patients' private rooms.

"He's a bit more out of sorts than usual today. Went back to his room after breakfast. We don't hassle him. We keep looking in to make sure he's okay. We don't lock him in." Darren paused before an anonymous pale green door. "This is him." He knocked. "Michael – it's Darren. I've someone to see you."

There was no response. Darren knocked again.

"A visitor for you, Michael!"

More silence.

"Michael – I'm coming in!"

He entered with Paul close behind. Paul found himself in a functional, but tastefully- furnished sitting room. French windows overlooked lawned gardens, where a scattering of residents strolled in the summer sunshine.

Michael Oliver sat in a leather Chesterfield armchair in the centre of the room, with a jagged splinter of wood projecting from his right eye.

"Oh my God! Don't look, Reverend Milton." Darren's voice was choked with shock. "I'll get help."

He rushed from the room, leaving Paul staring at the body in the chair. Michael Oliver, shaven and shorn and cleaner, looked surprised, as if he had just been the recipient of unexpected good news. There was very little blood. The splinter of wood had been so accurately directed that the brain had stopped functioning instantly and the heart soon after. The dead man's hands still rested on the arms of the chair. They had not been raised in self-defence, as though death had come so suddenly he had no time even to blink.

A painting hung on the wall directly opposite Michael Oliver's chair: a grove of oaks, like those in the churchyard at Low Moor. But, instead of a church, a vivid little spring flowed through an outcrop of anthropomorphic rocks in the centre ground. In the background was a view of dark moorland skylines. The grasses and trees had a strange swirling quality, like the paintings in the vicarage attic. The signature in the bottom left-hand corner read *Olwen Williams.*

Paul noticed that one of the oak trees in the foreground had a fresh-looking broken-off branch. He touched the split end of the branch. The paint was wet.

One of the French windows was slightly open. He looked out, just in time to spot two figures, monklike in their loose-fitting garb, disappearing among the trees at the far side of the gardens. If it hadn't been for their blond hair he would never have seen them. Their brown habits merged with the dappled background of sunlit trees, making them almost invisible.

* * *

Sarah rummaged around in the buildings that lined three sides of the cobbled stableyard at the back of the vicarage. She found nothing of any use and was about to give up when she spotted an old bicycle almost completely hidden behind a stack of damaged urns and plant pots. The tyres were flat, but responded to her vigorous efforts with the pump. She pushed the bike across the yard and out of the back gate.

She cycled through Low Moor village, smiling and waving at everyone she met. No-one smiled or waved back, just stared at her, as she told Paul later, as if she was dressed like a cartoon chicken. Undeterred she arrived at the small village store, propped her bike against the wall and breezed into the shop.

Three local women, in their mid-forties and dressed in practical outdoors' garb, chatted to the shop assistant at the counter. Sarah rushed towards them.

"Morning! I'm Sarah Milton. Paul, my husband, is your new vicar. He hopes you'll come to church on Sunday, where you'll all be very welcome. You must call to see us at the vicarage any time. Paul and I want to be friends to everyone in the parish!"

Her ebullient outburst met with complete silence.

One of the women gave her a sardonic smile. "Sorry, luv, seems we've gone and lost our faith." Her northern accent was similar to Arthur's, but a shade coarser.

A second woman shook her head in mock concern. "The vicars that 'ave come 'ere 'ave been *so* erratic."

The third woman laughed. "You see, they come. Then they die or go mad. And the church is locked up again for ages. So what's the point of botherin'?"

"Well, we're not erractic!" Sarah countered.

"Sorry, luv," the first speaker replied, "I think we're happy not being Christians these days."

"We've got into the way of doin' our own thing," the second woman explained. "And we'd quite like to carry on doin' it." There was a hint of hostility in the woman's voice.

The third woman laughed. "It's all gardenin' and sex with us – we really don't 'ave time for anythin' else!"

Sarah was taken aback. Her upbeat manner evaporated. "How did they die?" she asked earnestly. "How did the vicars die?"

The local women shook their heads and left without saying another word. Sarah, her anxiety rising, turned to the shop assistant.

"Can you tell me what happened to them?"

The shop assistant pulled a dismissive face. "You should ask that fellow Dodds. He's the only one who knows the whole of it."

Sarah rode back from the store with two cartons of milk she felt obliged to buy. The local women were talking on the village green.

"Bye! See you again soon!"

The women ignored her.

Sarah rode on. "You will accept us. You will!" she muttered under her breath. But her intuition told her a different story.

By the time she reached the vicarage she was in tears.

* * *

Arthur worked in the churchyard cutting the grass between the gravestones. Paul strode purposefully towards him. Arthur stopped the strimmer.

"Good day, Reverend Milton," he said cheerfully. "Did you find Reverend Oliver improved?"

"I found him murdered, Arthur! If I wasn't blessed with common sense, I'd call it death by psychokinesis!"

"And what does your common sense say?" Arthur asked, visibly shaken.

"It says I should start asking difficult questions – like who'd want to kill a poorly vicar?"

"Mebbe someone who's got no more use for him," Arthur replied enigmatically.

Before Paul could question him further Arthur re-started the strimmer and continued cutting grass. Paul, disturbed, made his way through the gate into the vicarage garden. Arthur, looking worried, stared after him.

* * *

The first-floor study contained a dozen shelves of old religious books arranged along two walls. The other walls of the narrow room were occupied by the door and large sash window. A workworn desk and bentwood chair occupied the centre of the room. The floor was of polished wood of a pleasingly varied tone. A faded Persian rug covered the area beneath the desk.

Paul swept in determinedly. He moved the desk under the window and sat in the bentwood chair looking out at the cobbled yard and the woods of Walden. He unpacked a small case and took out prayer books, a bible, hymn books and files of sermons, which he arranged systematically on the desk.

He rolled up the Persian rug, catching his finger on a loose floorboard beneath. He knelt down to investigate. The board had not been nailed to the joists and lifted out easily. He peered into the dark space beneath, felt around and pulled out a blank brown envelope.

The envelope contained a booklet entitled *A History of St Martin's Church, Walden.* The author's name was Edmund Reason and the date of publication was 1909. Inside the front cover were the hand-written words *Joan Preston. Durham. 1985.*

He replaced the floorboard, put the Persian rug back over it, sat at the desk and began to read the booklet.

Chapter Five

Paul and Sarah sat at the dining room table eating a simple evening meal. Neither seemed enthusiastic about food and pushed their plates away half finished.

"Sorry you had a bad day," he began, studying her for signs of stress.

She pulled a resigned face. "I'll get over it. At least they didn't become angry or make threats." She sighed. "But they'll be hard to win back. How did your day go?"

"It was mixed." He paused. As much as he would have liked to talk to her about Michael Oliver, past experience made him feel it was unwise. Sarah was far too highly strung to cope with a murder – certainly not one so close to their new lives. He held up the *St Martin's* booklet. This, he felt, was safer ground.

"I found this hidden in the study. It's about the ruined church up in Walden – back when it was a functioning place of worship."

"Why was it hidden? Is it blasphemous?"

He laughed. "No, not at all. But it is interesting. I've marked a few passages because they're quite intriguing. The first bit's from the diary of a past incumbent called William Grove, describing the strange events that happened in 1760. D'you want me to read it?"

She smiled eagerly. "Of course. You make it sound exciting!"

He smiled at her warmly and opened the booklet. He began to read:

"Last Sunday I did have the cross in St Martin's churchyard broken up. Upon my soul, this drastic step was the only way to prevent it being defiled."

"How do you defile a cross?" she interrupted, puzzled.

"The booklet doesn't say exactly why, but I imagine nonconformists had been preaching from it. Some of them were incredibly outspoken, accusing bishops and the clergy of corruption and self-interest. And also challenging them on points of doctrine. It happened all over England, particularly in the north."

"Is there more?"

"Oh, yes!" He continued reading:

"I am now the most abject man on earth, in fear for my life and sanity. Vile manifestations hold sway here, as hideous to look upon as they are fiendish in intent."

"Vile manifestations! What on earth could they be?" She seemed both intrigued and alarmed.

"I have to admit I've really no idea. Perhaps the village people burned an effigy of the poor vicar, or subjected him to some kind of skimmington ride. But I'm guessing. Whatever they were they must have been frightening and William Grove must have believed in them." He paused again to gauge her level of interest. "Shall I go on? There's another bit, from the Parish Book, written by a later incumbent, one Thomas Marshall, in 1857."

"Yes, go on," she enthused. "Please."

He continued reading from the booklet:

"I have this day dismissed the choirs of both my churches due to the evil spirit of opposition that resides in this place–"

"My goodness!" she exclaimed. "These are strong words, aren't they?"

He glanced at her across the table. "There's just this last bit. From Thomas Marshall again." He began reading, wondering if it had been a bad idea to mention the booklet at all:

"The people do not heed my words. They mock me and insult me and I dare not leave the vicarage."

"It sounds like a state of open rebellion!" She looked at him in wide-eyed wonder.

"I suppose it does. And against the authority of the Church, no less."

"Those people must have been dangerous. The vicars sound genuinely afraid."

"Well, from what I've read these northern nonconformists were a pretty wild lot. They were lawless times back then in rural England."

"If you're going up to Walden maybe I should come with you?"

He laughed. "It's just a ruin now. Those times have gone. The danger's over – I don't think I'll need a bodyguard!"

* * *

As Paul drove north through the country lanes he had the disconcerting impression that the wooded hillsides ahead of him were aware of his approach. The further he went the more overbearingly oppressive the woods seemed to become. He felt his chest tightening, his breathing becoming laboured. It was irrational nonsense, he told himself. But the symptoms persisted.

He had dressed informally, feeling the sight of a clerical collar might win him few friends among – what he assumed – were the left-brain atheists of Walden. Now he felt he'd have been better off carrying a supply of oxygen. He regretted making light of not needing a bodyguard. If Arthur had been with him at least he'd have had someone to talk with and to help dissipate the dark foreboding that was beginning to creep over him.

The road had narrowed to a single-track lane, which added to his sense of oppression. The woods crowded in tightly on both sides, their branches interlocking above him shutting out the light, so it felt as if he was driving through a tunnel. He made a mental note of the distances between passing places, but he saw no other vehicles. At last he came upon the village sign: *WALDEN. NO THROUGH ROAD.* The sign was almost unreadable beneath moss and spattered mud.

He approached a T-junction, pulled into a lay-by and got out. The right fork followed the thickly-wooded valley, the other led to a ruined church, whose roofless silhouette could be glimpsed against the sky on the edge of the moorland half a mile away.

This was his other church, the ruined *St Martin's*, the focus of much of the conflict described in the booklet. The sight of the ruin inspired a feeling of trepidation.

The purpose of his trip was to meet the residents of Walden more than to visit a ruined church, however important that might be, so he set off on foot into the wooded valley.

As he strode down the lane he felt the oppressive atmosphere lift a little. He could breathe more easily and his muzzy head had cleared. To his surprise he found he was enjoying his walk. He had the fleeting impression his emotions were being manipulated, but he could make no sense of the notion and quickly dismissed it.

Although he couldn't consider himself a genuine countryman he was impressed by the appearance of the landscape around him. Massive ancient trees lined both sides of the lane. Small fields and fruit-filled orchards appeared in gaps between the trees. He took note of the crops: potatoes, beans, Brussels sprouts, apples, pears, plums, all apparently flourishing. Goats were tethered by tall hedgesides and bleated at him as he passed. Hens scratched and skittered everywhere.

At last he caught glimpses of cottages among the trees. Old stone walls and slab roofs caught the light that filtered through the branches. A playful breeze picked up and made the laneside grasses shudder and swirl.

He arrived at a well-trodden track that led off the lane towards an old cottage, whose mellow stonework glowed in the sunlight. He approached the front door, which stood wide open. He knocked. There was no response. He stepped into the house.

He entered a living room full of old-fashioned furniture: robust sideboards, a Welsh dresser, heavy table and chairs – all made, he assumed, from the local oak.

"Hello!" he called. "Anyone home?"

There was no response. He was about to leave when cats of all sizes and colours materialised, as it seemed, from nowhere. They leaped on to the table, the chairs and the dresser. Surprised, he took a step backwards and felt more cats brushing against his legs.

For a moment he was unsure what to do. Should he call out again or retreat and try another cottage? His decision was promptly made for him.

The cats sprang at him, hissing and spitting. They leaped at his face, clinging to his back and shoulders, howling and moaning with rising intensity. He fended them off the best he could and ran from the room.

No sooner had he left the cottage than the door slammed shut behind him. He closed his eyes and offered up a silent prayer of thanks for his escape. He decided to make his way back to the lane, but to his dismay he could see no sign of the track he had followed to the cottage door.

The trees around him appeared more numerous, massive, ancient and threatening. They seemed to press in on him, hollows in their trunks becoming transformed into mouths and eyes, branches swaying and rattling like bones in the rising wind. Fallen leaves swirled into his face. He stumbled and fell, got up and struggled on. He fought his way through the unyielding limbs until, to his relief, he reached the lane.

He looked back. Three cats watched him from the edge of the trees. He stared at them, unnerved. They arched their backs and spat at him.

* * *

Shaken he walked slowly up the lane between mature stands of Scots pine and birch. The ruined church was ahead of him with open moorland beyond. The lane ended abruptly at the churchyard wall, with no turning space for a vehicle. He deduced from this single fact there had been no service here for the best part of a century. Edmund Reason, the author of the *St Martin's* booklet, had simply said the place was "in decay" in the early 1900s.

In the churchyard wall was a gate, by the side of which was a time-worn board fixed to a stout post. On the board were the faded words *St Martin's*. He opened the gate and entered the churchyard. Ancient gravestones leaned among long grass. He noted an old cross base that occupied the corner of the churchyard and imagined wild nonconformist preachers waving their fists at the terrified Reverend Grove.

Though much smaller than All Saints church in Low Moor, he could see at once that St Martin's was built in the same Early English Gothic style, with pointed arches and simple lancet windows. All that work and hope, he thought, to end like this.

He was surprised to see Olwen Williams painting at an easel set among the gravestones. She smiled and gave him a little wave.

"Hi again."

"Hi. Just come up for a look at my other church."

He was tempted to approach her, curious to see how she might paint a Christian subject, but he checked himself and went into the church. He failed to notice Olwen's hostile glance as he entered the ruined porch.

Stepping from the porch into the nave he found himself in an empty space. No debris on the floor. No cracked and battered font. Only a little ivy covering the lower walls. The place was remarkably clean, as if the floor had been recently swept. But the state of the floor was soon forgotten when he looked up at the tower arch.

It was an unorthodox equilateral arch, unusually high for a church with a relatively short tower. Seven huge carved heads adorned it. Grotesque and sinister, they were completely free from ivy and from any trace of mould. The central head was a Giant, grasping its jaws with both hands, pulling its open mouth into a savage gaping grimace. A small half-swallowed naked figure disappeared head first between the Giant's teeth.

To one side of the Giant was the head of a Cernunnos-like horned god, with writhing serpents issuing from its mouth. On the other side was the head of a Green Man, with foliage sprouting from its mouth and ears.

On both sides of this trinity were pairs of ferocious demons, with glaring eyes and bared fangs.

He stared at the heads on the tower arch in astonishment. He had seen graphic church carvings before in pre-Reformation churches – monstrous gargoyles and the occasional demon or gryphon as at Low Moor, sometimes a lewd monk or a bishop with a fox's head – but never anything like these.

They were awesome. And they were also indisputably the work of pagans.

He caught sight of Olwen through an unglazed lancet window. She seemed preoccupied, busy at her easel. He turned away, not wishing to spy. But, as he did so, he thought he heard laughter from the churchyard. His curiosity aroused, he turned to look again...

Olwen in her younger form leaned seductively against a gravestone. She was naked and in the act of caressing her breasts.

He gasped with shock and turned away. But, before he had time to get himself under control, he found himself looking again. Olwen was painting at her easel as before. She looked up and saw him, meeting his guilty gaze with a small discerning smile.

He leaned against the nave wall, his mind in a state of whirling confusion. Was she doing this or was he? He couldn't believe the former, because that implied her mastery of some kind of metaphysical power, but the latter was just as unacceptable. He had a loyal wife. He had never felt attracted to another woman. What poisoned cup had he drunk from to be suddenly a prey to this?

After a half-hearted glance at the chancel he stepped from the church. He was about to leave the churchyard, but felt an irresistible urge to speak with Olwen. He waded through the long grasses towards her.

"Those heads," he began, "I'm surprised they've survived. They're so blatantly pagan."

She smiled at him, slightly mischievously, he thought. "Oh, so many vicars tried to remove them. Obviously they all failed."

"Why do you think that was?" he asked, genuinely anxious to know more.

"Someone must have wanted to keep them," she replied enigmatically.

"Who could have achieved that against the wishes of a bishop?"

"Perhaps the people of Walden had a powerful benefactor."

She smiled mysteriously. He found her gaze was unsettling him and he was losing the thread of his thoughts. With an effort he forced himself to concentrate.

"D'you know why this place was abandoned?"

"There's too much reality here," she replied, looking at him with large serious eyes.

He had another question ready on his tongue, but he lost the gist of it. He felt distracted by her presence and also by the painting, which kept catching his eye. It showed the church and churchyard, but the grass had begun to morph out of its physical form to become swirls of energy, as if it was dancing in the wind. Although he hadn't liked the paintings of hers he had seen at the vicarage, this one was not displeasing, the colours and textures creating a much lighter effect.

"I've seen paintings of yours at the vicarage."

"Michael collected them. He was quite a fan. How is he, by the way?"

The question seemed to be asked in all innocence. She was obviously on first-name terms with the man, so they must have been good friends.

"Michael Oliver's dead, I'm afraid," he stated matter-of-factly.

"Oh – the poor soul! Julius Dodds doesn't have much luck with his vicars, does he?"

"You know Reverend Dodds?" he asked, surprised.

Her manner changed abruptly. She almost spat the words at him. "Dodds is a murdering criminal! You should have nothing to do with that man!"

"He's a man of God!" he replied, shocked and angry.

"He's no more a Christian than that cloud in the sky, or that tree in the earth!" she stated emphatically.

"What grounds can you possibly have for saying that?" he retorted hotly, completely astounded.

"I know him," she said quietly. "He believes only in power – and in getting his own way."

"I can't accept that! It's not true!" He found himself shouting in Dodds's defence. Or – the thought occurred to him – was it, in fact, in his own?

"You'll find out the truth before very long. I pity you." She put her hand on his arm and gazed at him. "Let me paint you. I see great inner strength and compassion. I'd like to capture an impression of that."

"No!" he blurted out. "I have duties. I must go."

"Another time, perhaps." She squeezed his arm and smiled.

He hurried to the churchyard gate, then turned and looked back. Olwen had morphed into her younger form. She exposed her breasts and tossed her raven curls.

* * *

Paul drove slowly in the direction of Low Moor. Nothing like this had ever happened to him before. He had looked at attractive women on a thousand occasions, without spontaneously undressing them and imagining them performing lewd acts.

He was becoming ill. There was no denying it. And the root cause was his relationship with Sarah. She was too volatile, he reasoned, even to the point of being emotionally unstable.

In London he'd had to struggle with her, as much as he had to work hard to win a congregation. One day she was the model wife: supportive, innovative and full of positive energy. The next she would be moody, uncooperative, even hostile. On those days she was best left alone, or arguments would inevitably flare up.

But it wasn't a solid bedrock from which to confront lapsed Christians. And since her mother's death she had grown more extreme. She was driving him away from her, no doubt of it.

But was he also guilty? Was he indulging in an ego-trip for God at the expense of his humanity? And what kind of God accepted fanatics, with all their intolerance, as His servants? Answer: a cruel God, a jealous God, a–

His thoughts were suddenly interrupted. As he passed the sign *WALDEN. NO THROUGH ROAD* he noticed two locals sitting in a potato field by the side of the lane. They were slumped against each other, as if asleep.

He skidded to a sudden stop, reversed quickly, jumped out of the car and ran to the two slumped figures. Something was wrong about them. He'd seen similar figures in London's derelict warehouses and in the stairwells of rundown tower blocks...

They were dead. It seemed as if their necks had been broken. On their foreheads was the branded mark of a cross.

He recoiled in horror and whipped out his mobile, with the intention of calling the emergency services, but there was no signal.

Then he spotted two brown-robed monks slipping away through nearby trees.

"Hey!" he yelled. "HEY!!"

The monks ignored him. He chased after them, searching among the trees, but he was unable to find them. It was as if they had dematerialised, their habits making them almost invisible.

He caught a brief impression of movement – it was the monks, making their way through dense undergrowth a hundred yards away. He charged after them among the gnarled trees, fighting his way through tangles of branches and roots. He spotted them again some distance ahead, moving quickly away through more open woodland.

"Hey! Come back here! Stop! Stop will you!"

The monks took no notice, moving quickly away.

A sudden heavy rain shower lashed at him. Visibility was dramatically reduced. He lost sight of the monks. Though he cast around he could find no further sign of them. He gave up the pursuit. Wet through, he returned to his car.

The rain stopped. A little way off, behind a screen of bushes, the two monks watched him.

Chapter Six

Sarah cycled through the sunny summer lanes of Walden. She passed well-tended gardens, orchards laden with nuts and fruit. Villagers of all ages worked in the fields. They waved to her. She waved back happily. Walden seemed like a friendly place after her frosty reception in Low Moor.

Paul had left her alone in the vicarage, with nothing to do except help Beryl in the kitchen garden. But she had her bike now and it was ideal weather to ride out to Walden and get to know the local countryside. Paul couldn't expect her to be a prisoner in the vicarage. In London she had gone out whenever she felt like it – and there had always been someone interesting to meet, especially in the street markets.

During their almost four years of marriage things had changed. She had seen her husband become more and more obsessive in his devotion to the church. At times it had seemed as if she hardly existed. They had ended up running quite a busy church, but it was all *Reverend Paul this* and *Paul that.* It seemed she was only required to play the piano and organise jumble sales.

This new rural position was a welcome change – and she was determined to use it to make a life for herself. She thought she would spend more of her time in Walden as the people seemed as if they might be more responsive.

Olwen, Rhiannon, Gwenda, Gareth and Rhys were picking red plums in an orchard. There was a lot of laughter as they chased each other around the trees. Olwen, looking benign and motherly, waved to Sarah as she cycled by. Sarah pulled up and watched them wistfully.

"Sarah!" Olwen called. "Come and join the fun!"

Sarah couldn't resist the invitation. She left her bike on the verge and hurried into the orchard. Olwen and her companions moved away among the trees. Sarah, excited, chased after them. They called to her teasingly.

"Sarah!"

"Catch me, Sarah!"

"Quick, Sarah, quick!"

Gareth let her catch him. Rhys pulled her away. Gareth pulled her back in a gentle tug of war. As she passed from one to the other they stroked her in an increasingly intimate way. The three women joined them and began to caress each other. In no time at all they were lying in the orchard grass and kissing. Sarah hadn't felt so excited since she was a child – and, she had to admit, so sexually stimulated in all her adult life. She rolled in the grass with Gareth and laughed. After a while Olwen pulled her to her feet.

"What a game! Sarah – meet Rhiannon, Gwenda, Gareth and Rhys."

They all took Sarah's hands, stroked her hair and kissed her.

Gareth laughed. "Come again, pretty Sarah!"

Rhys kissed her tenderly on the cheek. "Whenever you like!"

Sarah laughed and laughed. Her new friends smiled at her fondly.

* * *

Paul pulled in fast through the vicarage gates and leaped from the Fiesta. Arthur was busy weeding the flower beds that edged the lawn. Paul rushed up to him.

"There's been a murder in Walden! I must get the police!"

He turned to run into the house.

"Reverend Milton."

Arthur's tone stopped Paul in his tracks.

"Did they have the mark of a cross burned into their foreheads?"

Arthur's voice had taken on an added depth of solemnity.

"They did," Paul replied curtly. "And can you tell me what brings the Inquisition to the fields and lanes of Walden?"

"My advice to you, Reverend Milton, is to leave this matter alone," Arthur stated sombrely. "Don't get involved."

"But I think I saw the killers!" Paul objected.

"Don't interfere. For your own sake. And for your wife's."

"Interfere? This is murder!"

Paul turned towards the house, changed his mind, ran back to his car and drove out through the gates.

Arthur stared after him anxiously.

* * *

The nearest police station was almost twenty miles to the north, in a craggy valley on the other side of the moors. Paul burst in, but found the place deserted. His shouts attracted an irritable duty sergeant, who refused to listen to his excited outbursts and showed him to an interview room telling him to wait.

He sat at a table in the windowless room and tried to organise his thoughts. What had he seen? What indeed *had* he seen...? It all suddenly seemed so incredible he began to doubt the veracity of his experience. He made an effort to quieten his mind and pray, but words from *King Lear* sprang unsummoned into his head: *O! Let me not be mad, not mad, sweet heaven.* The words went round and round until he leaped to his feet and shouted *STOP!!*

A moment later a serious-looking young constable came in and sat at the table. The constable opened a notebook, laid it before himself, but made no attempt to write in it.

"You're the new vicar at Low Moor?" the constable began.

Paul resumed his seat. "I am."

"The sergeant mentioned you'd seen two dead bodies up at Walden," the constable continued matter-of-factly.

"I think their necks were broken," Paul replied. As the horrific images rose up into his mind his turmoil of doubt disappeared. How could he have imagined anything so grotesque?

"I see," the constable said, frowning. "We've received no reports of missing persons or of deaths in Walden, sir."

"No? Well I'm reporting one now," Paul replied. "Two deaths in fact."

"Thanks for taking the trouble to come in, sir." The constable switched on a smile approximating gratitude, then added, as if he was reading from a prepared script. "We'll certainly take every opportunity to look into it."

"They were in a potato field. I can take you straight there."

The constable turned on his photo-call smile. "That won't be necessary, sir. We'll deal with it. But thanks for your offer."

Paul could no longer control his irritation at what he felt was becoming a farce. "Look, constable, I saw the killers. They were leaving the scene."

"Did you see these alleged killers killing the alleged victims?" the constable asked.

"No...but I know it was them. I can give you a description."

"That's kind of you, sir, but we'll take it from here," the constable stated firmly.

Paul made what he felt was a final empty gesture: "I'd like to visit the families of the deceased and offer my condolences. It's my duty as their vicar."

"We have yet to establish that anyone has died, sir." The constable added what seemed to Paul no more than a hollow afterthought. "When we have proof we'll be in touch."

"There'll be an investigation, constable, surely?" Paul asked, beating off waves of despair.

The constable got to his feet. "Have no doubts about that, sir. We'll be as thorough as we have need to be. We'll send a car up right away and make enquiries." He picked up his empty notebook.

Paul stood up too. "Am I right in thinking this situation has happened before, constable?"

"I couldn't possibly make any comment on that, sir," the constable replied in a tone of finality.

* * *

Paul, having eluded two of the bishop's attendants by his nimble and determined footwork, found – more by luck than judgement – Hugh Mortimer in his shirt sleeves seated in his private sitting room. The bishop was watching a DVD of *The Sound of Music* and singing along loudly but slightly out of tune to *Climb Ev'ry Mountain.*

He stood up as Paul entered and tried to block the sight of the TV by placing his generous frame in front of it. He seemed to have misplaced the remote and the two men found themselves shouting above the strains of the song.

"Reverend Milton!" the bishop exclaimed.

"My Lord Bishop!" Paul replied. He spotted the remote protruding from beneath a cushion on the sofa, snatched it up and muted the DVD.

"This is my private time, Reverend Milton." The bishop stated, overcoming his initial embarrassment. "You should have made an appointment."

"Murdered farmers in Walden had an appointment, which ended with two broken necks! To my amazement the police showed no interest! What does the Church have to say?"

The bishop swallowed his shock. "Murdered?" he managed to blurt out.

"Precisely. By two of Dodds's heavies. What exactly is going on?"

The bishop's attendants appeared in the doorway. The bishop waved them away and indicated a chair.

"Please be seated, Reverend Milton. Let's talk like civilized men."

Paul and the bishop sat facing each other in wingback Lancaster armchairs. The bishop had regained his composure.

"You should speak with Reverend Dodds about this matter. The selection of incumbents for Low Moor and Walden is part of his duties, not mine."

"So you're abdicating responsibility for what happens in Walden?" Paul replied angrily.

"I'm simply pointing out that any problems you think you may have come across in Walden should be referred to Reverend –"

Paul was on his feet. "My Lord Bishop, I know what I saw! Someone must take responsibility! But it's obviously not going to be you!"

The bishp bristled. "I don't care for your tone, Reverend Milton!"

"And I don't care for yours!"

The bishop's attendants appeared in the doorway. They must have been summoned by a hidden device on the bishop's chair, Paul realised later.

The bishop stood up. "Reverend Milton is just leaving."

Paul ignored the attendants and walked from the room.

When he had gone the bishop resumed his armchair. For a long time he sat with eyes closed, an anguished expression taking hold of his features. The DVD of *The Sound of Music* continued playing silently in the background.

* * *

Paul sat by the window in the vicarage sitting room brooding on the events of the day. The more he replayed them the more the whole sequence felt like a dream.

There had been cats in the Walden cottage, he had claw marks on his jacket collar to prove it. And there had been two bodies in the field, he could not have invented them. The entire ambience of Walden unsettled him. It was as if different rules applied there and he was the only person who didn't understand what they were.

His thoughts were interrupted as Arthur came in with a basket of logs and placed it by the fireside.

"You'll need these, Reverend Milton. Nights are getting chilly."

Paul got to his feet and turned to face the churchwarden. "I can't make any sense of this, Arthur." He flung his hands in the air in a gesture of despair. "The attitude of the police suggests some sort of on-going crisis in Walden. I'm going to ring the bishop. I'll ask him to speak to the chief constable. I need to know what's happening – I'm the vicar of Walden too!"

Arthur looked troubled. "Please, Reverend Milton, don't stir things up. You'll make more problems for yourself."

Exasperation drove Paul across the room. He faced Arthur furiously. "What's going on, Arthur? Were those farmers the victims of a civil war battle re-enactment that went wrong? Or was it, as I think it was, calculated murder?"

Arthur seemed to be struggling against an overwhelming reluctance to reply. He overcame it at last, merely out of politeness, Paul felt, more than any sense of moral obligation.

"Just observe, Reverend Milton. Don't react. That's the best way to find out what's happening here." Arthur suddenly looked helpless even, Paul thought, a little scared. "Talk to Dodds. He knows everything. Please, I can't answer any more questions."

When Arthur had gone Paul read his prayer book by a brightly-burning fire. He read the words, but they had lost all meaning.

Images of dead locals and brown-robed monks tore at his emotions and paralysed his intellect. As he put the book unhappily aside Sarah bounded in, radiant and over-excited.

"What a wonderful place!" she exclaimed.

"What is?" he asked, confused.

"Walden, of course! It's so beautiful and fruitful! Those people really are in tune with nature. I've never seen such laden orchards this far north!"

She flopped into an armchair. He suppressed his alarm.

"How was your day," she asked brightly. "Did you see St Martin's church?"

He wrestled with his emotions, momentarily stuck for words.

"Beryl was at the weekly market and said she saw you leaving the police station. Did you witness a crime?"

The word *crime* focused his thoughts. "I think we should talk about Walden," he managed.

"Talk? Whatever for?" she laughed. "It's great up there! Enjoy it!"

"It's not the way it seems," he replied tersely.

"Nonsense. What's wrong with you today?" she asked indignantly.

He couldn't speak. He felt wracked with confusion and anxiety. What could he say to her? He was unable to explain the day's events to himself. She was so happy. He hadn't seen her like this since the first weeks of their marriage. He couldn't bring himself to destroy her mood.

But he must. He had no choice.

She seemed oblivious of his conflict. She bounced to her feet. "Going for a bath. Got seeds in my shoes and leaves in my hair." She swept from the room.

He hesitated, then rushed to the door.

"Saraaaah!"

But she had already disappeared upstairs.

* * *

Paul entered their bedroom in his boxer shorts with a glass of milk. Sarah was reading in bed. She put her book aside.

"Going to start our little family?"

"Little?" he asked warily.

She laughed. "Three."

She flung back the covers and pulled him into bed. He loosened up and started to laugh. She began to caress him.

He saw Olwen in her younger form, naked and in sexual arousal, reflected in the dressing table mirror. Olwen seemed to be staring straight at him as she touched her breasts.

"No!" he cried in alarm. "NO!!"

He wrenched himself out of bed and flung milk from his half-drunk glass at the mirror. The milk obliterated Olwen's image.

Sarah sat up in dismay. "Paul – whatever's wrong?"

"Moths!" he replied, fearful and confused.

"Moths?" she repeated. "Have you gone crazy?"

He turned back to her, his emotions spinning in free fall. But it was Olwen he saw in Sarah's place in the bed. "Get away!" he yelled. "GET AWAAAAY!"

He leaped at Olwen and began to strangle her. Olwen vanished. He removed his trembling hands from Sarah's neck.

"Ouch! You hurt me." She rubbed her neck. "Have you gone completely mad? Are you trying to invent some new sexual game?"

"Sorry," he blurted. "I was... overreacting."

He sat on the edge of the bed, his head in his hands.

"What's the matter now?" she said crossly. "Aren't we going to have sex? You seemed as if you wanted to."

He shook his head. "I can't."

* * *

Reverend Dodds, engaged in the exorcism of All Saints church, stood before the altar, on which four candles were placed, one at each corner. Two monks assisted.

"*From the deceits and crafts of the Evil One, O Lord deliver us. That it may please Thee to rule Thy Church in lasting peace and true liberty, We beseech Thee, hear us.*"

He raised his cross. The monks sprinkled holy water from phials around the altar.

Paul, looking haggard and having omitted his morning shave, stepped into the chancel. "Murderers!" he roared. "I shall make a citizen's arrest!"

He tried to grab the nearest monk. Before he could lay a hand on him the monk had thrown him face down on the floor, placing his knee in Paul's back, his hands around his forehead, about to jerk back his head and break his neck.

"Enough!"

At Dodds's command the monk let Paul go. He scrambled to his feet.

"Get out of the church!" Paul cried. "I won't have killers under this sacred roof!"

"We're not answerable to you, Reverend Milton." Dodds pronounced icily.

"To whom, then?" Paul asked angrily.

"To God. And to God alone." Dodds replied.

"God!? You work for God?" Paul bellowed in dismay. "Your hypocrisy staggers me!"

"You're seriously mistaken here, I think." Dodds stated quietly.

"I am not mistaken!" Paul yelled, affronted by the man's dismissive attitude. "I saw your assassins running away! What kind of Christian kills innocent potato farmers?"

"There's no such thing as innocence in Walden, Reverend Milton!" Dodds thundered.

"What's that supposed to mean?" Paul asked hotly.

"You'll find out – and very soon! If you must know I'm a reclaimer of souls. Of those who have slipped from the path. And there are many such in Walden. I've been assigned the task of retrieving them."

"Assigned?" Paul asked, incredulous. "By whom?"

"I am not at liberty to say." Reverend Dodds glared threateningly at Paul. "And certainly not to a *vicar*."

The word *vicar* was pronounced with more distaste than Paul had ever heard in his life. Dodds's contempt fuelled his outrage – he was not going to leave this so-called *reverend* in any doubt about his feelings.

"This is my benefice!" Paul asserted coolly but firmly. "Leave me to do my job!"

"I'm here simply to exorcise the church." Dodds's eyes seemed to bore into Paul's face like weapons. "There are malevolent forces here. Watch and learn." He turned to the two monks. "Go about your work."

A monk sprinkled holy water around the chancel. Dismayed, Paul watched as small winged demons, in superficial appearance part toad, part bat, fled from beneath the pews and tried to fly up to the dark corners of the roof. Before they could escape the second monk produced a crossbow, dipped his arrow-barbs in a phial of sulphur and shot them down.

The demons shrieked horribly and shrivelled up in a burst of smoke, dropping to the floor like disgusting rags.

The two monks picked them up on the points of their knives and tossed the remains in a sack.

Paul watched the proceedings in horror. "What kind of foul witchery is this?" he demanded.

"You see, don't you? You have eyes?" Dodds flung the words at Paul like lethal elf shot. "They are merely low spirits. We're fortunate. Wait till we're fighting soul displacers!"

"I'll report you to the bishop for conjuring devils!" Paul stated threateningly.

"Report away, Reverend Milton! The bishop will be amused by you, I think." He paused, studying Paul darkly. "And there's no point going to the palace shouting and issuing ultimatums. Be advised: you will be putting your own future at risk."

Paul could hardly believe his ears. "Are you threatening me?"

"You must read into my words what you will," Dodds replied.

"Why do you want me here?" Paul asked. "Is it just for appearances?"

"I require you to be my eyes and ears in the parishes."

"A spy?" Paul asked in dismay.

"Yes, a spy if you like. You must be vigilant and on your guard at all times. Divide and rule is the aim of that Walden cult."

"Just what is going on here, Dodds?" Paul asked, his anger rising again.

"Surely it's obvious, Reverend Milton?" Dodds glared at Paul in cold condescension. "We're at war!" He made a sweeping gesture around the church. "You'll find the atmosphere in here much improved now, I think."

Reverend Dodds and the two monks, carrying their sack of dead demons, strode from the church.

Paul sank on to a pew, suddenly exhausted. He felt his sense of reality, whatever that had been, slipping beyond recall.

Chapter Seven

Paul hurried through the gate into St Martin's churchyard. An empty easel stood among the gravestones and long grass. There was no sign of Olwen. He walked among the gravestones, reading the names of the departed: *Pugh, Jones, Davies, Evans, Hughes, Williams, Owen...*

He paused and pondered. All these were Welsh names. No Saxons or Norsemen. Then he realised: Walden – the Valley of the Welsh. A Celtic enclave. And Olwen Williams its pagan priestess.

He found two fresh unmarked graves, with offerings of flowers, fruit and vegetables arranged at one end. He stared down at them, wondering if Dodds and his monkish thugs had been successful in reclaiming the souls of these unfortunate locals. The church and churchyard had not been deconsecrated, but the burial rites had doubtless been pagan. So who were the winners? He had no clear answers.

Going into the ruined church he stood beneath the carved heads on the tower arch. His gaze settled on the central head, that of the Giant. He stared hard at the open mouth, with the naked figure in its jaws about to disappear, as if the intensity of his focus might elucidate the mystery that surrounded him.

Before he had time to prevent it his perception seemed to detach itself like a separate active force and fly through the giant's mouth into darkness. The darkness became a swirling centrifuge of energy, sucking his perception inwards with irresistible power. It seemed to

Paul that his entire non-physical being was spinning with the energy like a tiny craft in a maelstrom.

Then, suddenly, a sound. Or, more accurately, a vibration. At first faint, then stronger. A pulse swelling like a booming drum until it seemed to be the only sound left in the world. At first he couldn't accept what his intelligence was telling him. It was impossible that he should be picking up a vibration like the pulsing of a heart.

He burst from the ruined porch, flailing his arms, fighting for breath. He was sweating profusely, his features strained with terror. He leaned against the churchyard wall, his eyes closed, slowly regaining his composure. What was it, he asked himself, what *was* it he had experienced? The drumming of his own blood, surely. What else could it possibly be?

He didn't hear her enter the churchyard but, when he opened his eyes, Olwen in her maternal form was standing in front of him.

"You look as if you've had a shock," she said, in a tone that seemed like genuine concern.

For a moment he was too surprised to speak. Then a torrent of anger surged through him. "Why are you harassing me?" he shouted. "What have I done to hurt you? Why can't you leave me alone to get on with my life?"

She smiled at him, unperturbed. "You want the truth?" She didn't wait for his reply. "This –" she made a sweeping gesture at the church and churchyard – "this was once ours, a sanctuary of the Old Religion. The Christians stole it. They stole all the ancient sacred places. And the people were weak. They allowed themselves to be tricked, rather than rising up and throwing the Christians into the sea." She looked at Paul with an expression of pity. "Do you want to work for a bunch of thieves? I can offer you true enlightenment. What has Dodds given you? A vicarage – and slavery!"

"I'm no-one's slave!" he yelled. "I'm a free man!"

"Dodds requires obedience," she replied calmly. "I call that slavery."

She turned away from him, morphing into her younger self. She turned back and seized hold of his hands. "Forget Dodds. Come to me. We'll have such a time, you and I!"

Before he could collect himself his resolve was swept aside. They embraced each other passionately. They kissed and tore at each other's clothes...

He suddenly pulled back.

"NO!!" He fended her off. "I lead my life according to my beliefs, not yours!"

"But they told you what to believe, didn't they, priest?" She uttered a short harsh laugh. "And you fell for it!"

"No!" he said angrily. "I make up my own mind about all things!"

He glared at her. His emotions in turmoil he rushed from the churchyard.

She returned to her older form, watched him hurrying away down the lane and smiled.

* * *

Sarah cycled quickly through the lanes of Walden. She stopped beneath the overhanging branch of an apple tree, looked around to make sure she was not being watched, then helped herself to an apple. She bit into it, savouring its sweet juices.

Rhiannon stepped from the trees. "They're not quite ready. You should try the ones in the other orchard." She laughed at Sarah's guilty features. "Come, be with us. Enjoy yourself."

Olwen, Sarah, Rhiannon, Gwenda, Rhys and Gareth picked apples in a nearby orchard.

Sarah looked around at the laden trees. "I love it here. Such a pity the whole world isn't like this."

Olwen smiled at her tenderly. "Don't worry. Your sadness will soon be cured."

"How do you know I'm sad?" Sarah asked.

"Older women can tell." Olwen's expression was kindly, but serious. "You lost someone close to you quite recently, didn't you?"

"How did you know?" Sarah asked in surprise. "It was my mother. Almost a year ago."

Olwen studied Sarah's face intently. Although she didn't ask any more questions, her sympathetic manner seemed to invite further confidences.

"It was a joyrider," Sarah said eventually. "It was such a pointless death. How could it happen in God's world? My husband forgave the young man. But I can't." She wept a little, she couldn't help it. "I miss her so much." She took a photograph from her shoulder bag and showed it to Olwen. "I carry this everywhere."

Olwen studied the photograph. Her attention seemed to focus on it like a force of nature. "She looks like a lovely person," she said at last. "I can understand why you miss her."

Gareth took Sarah's hand. "Poor Sarah. And God didn't help."

"I think he's become so remote he doesn't relate to people," Gwenda said sadly. "He's cut himself off from us. He doesn't really care."

"But we're here now." Rhiannon stroked Sarah's hair.

"And we do care." Rhys took Sarah's other hand.

They embraced and kissed Sarah in turn.

"We're always here for you, Sarah," Olwen smiled. "You know that now, don't you?"

Sarah smiled back at them through tears of gratitude.

Some distance away, on elevated ground, Reverend Dodds watched the scene through binoculars. Two monks with crossbows stood behind him, their eyes shifting warily over the surrounding landscape, on the lookout for a surprise attack by locals.

Eventually Dodds lowered the binoculars and smiled with grim satisfaction. "Just as I thought." He glanced at his companions. "The witch has taken my bait. It won't be long before she starts her next offensive."

* * *

Olwen and Sarah were alone in the apple orchard. The light of the setting sun filtered through the leaves, touching the trees with a dappled golden glow. Sarah leaned against the low bough of an apple tree, as Olwen, seated on the grass, sketched her in a large sketch pad.

After a while Olwen got to her feet. "The light's fading." She closed her sketch pad. "I'll finish it later." She kissed Sarah on the forehead. "You're such a lovely girl. You seem almost like a daughter to me."

Sarah knew she was blushing at the unexpected compliment. "You've made me feel very welcome here. I've never experienced anything like it."

"Not everyone is welcome in Walden," Olwen replied with studied seriousness. "We prefer gentle and sensitive souls up here. People like ourselves." She indicated her sketch pad. "Can we agree that this will be our secret? I'd like it to be a surprise for your charming husband."

* * *

Paul drank tea by a log fire in the vicarage sitting room. He looked troubled and preoccupied. The *St Martin's* booklet lay open on the coffee table. Sarah breezed into the room.

"You're late," he snapped. He didn't turn around.

"So? I'm not a child!" she replied hotly. "I don't need a chaperone."

His manner softened. "I was worried."

"I've been with my friends in Walden. I was perfectly safe."

He sprang to his feet. "Keep away from Walden! It's dangerous! You must never go back there!"

She was taken aback by his vehemence. "Dangerous? How?"

He couldn't explain. What could he say that wouldn't terrify her, that wouldn't upset the already precarious state of her emotions? She might not even believe him. And then he would have to spell it all out, scene by macabre scene.

He would have to mention Olwen and her sexual advances, part of which, he now firmly believed, was the result of his own desires. His temptation was a private and personal cross he would have to bear, a situation he would have to work through.

No, it was impossible. He could say nothing more about Walden.

"I don't want to upset you," he managed at last. "Just take my word for it. Keep away from Walden. Please."

A furtive resentful look flitted across her face. "All right. You're the boss." She turned on her heel and stalked out of the room.

"We're a team!" he called after her, too late.

* * *

Paul lay in the four-poster bed. The events of the day had exhausted him and he slept soundly. Sarah, in a light sleep, moved restlessly. She woke with a start.

A figure in a shawl stood at the foot of the bed with its back to her. The figure, with bowed head, turned around. Sarah sat up, emitting a little startled cry.

"Mother! Oh, mother!"

Her mother raised her head and looked at her. "Hush, Sarah, dear. Be at peace. I'm so pleased for you. I know you have found a new friend. I have come to you to tell you that Olwen Williams will be a great comfort to you. She will be closer even than Paul. Listen to her. Take her advice in all things."

"Yes, mother. Thank you. I will." Sarah replied dutifully.

"I'm sorry I haven't been there for you," her mother continued. "But now you have found Olwen you will be happy at last."

Her mother faded and slowly disappeared.

"Mother! Mother! Please stay with me a bit longer!" Sarah cried, springing from the bed. But her mother had gone.

She sat on the bed, suddenly bereft, but also surprisingly elated. Paul stirred and woke up.

"Was it a nightmare?" he asked drowsily.

"It was nothing," she replied dismissively. "Go back to sleep."

Olwen sat by the fire in her basement. She stared into the flames. In her hand she held the photograph of Sarah's mother.

* * *

Paul, wearing his suit and clerical collar, parked his car in the cathedral precinct car park. He hurried towards a block of ecclesiastical buildings, attractively built in mellow eighteenth-century brick.

Ten minutes later he sat impatiently in the bishop's office, enduring the ritual of tea drinking and wondering why the bishop had summoned him.

"I trust you have recovered from your crisis, Reverend Milton," the bishop said with a solicitous smile, "and that you are settling in at last."

Paul's anger carried him to his feet. "No, My Lord Bishop, I'm afraid I have not recovered at all. What kind of Church is this that employs murderers? I'm stuck between Dodds's thugs and a village full of pagans! What am I supposed to do?"

He had chosen not to mention Olwen Williams. Her influence on him was a subjective matter that only he could resolve.

The bishop's smile slipped sideways a little, but seemed reluctant to depart entirely, giving his features a lop-sided appearance, as if he had been suddenly stricken with Bell's palsy.

"Every benefice has its individual challenges, Reverend Milton. We must accept them as a test of our faith. I'm sure you will be equal to this trial."

"But I'm certain I can never be," Paul replied. "Nothing in my life has prepared me for a situation like this. I must request a transfer."

The bishop sighed. "I'm afraid I have to refuse your request."

"I'll go to the press!" Paul said in desperation. "I'll tell them the truth of what's happening here!"

The bishop shook his head. "Do you think a scandal would alter anything in your parishes? I doubt that very much. I must ask you to exercise fortitude and restraint, Reverend Milton. Look what happened to poor Reverend Oliver."

"Are you threatening me?" Paul asked in angry surprise.

The bishop's face hardened slightly. "You're overwrought, Reverend Milton. Please calm yourself." He gestured to a chair. "Be seated, if you please."

Paul remained on his feet. The bishop studied him, like a headmaster might consider a talented but wayward pupil.

"Be assured, Reverend Milton," the bishop continued, "the Church will always support you."

"Like it supported Michael Oliver?" Paul retorted furiously. "Dodds had him removed to a private asylum!"

"I'm sure Reverend Oliver was in receipt of appropriate care." The bishop hurried on before Paul could raise more objections. "You should be guided by Reverend Dodds. He, not I, was responsible for your appointment."

"But surely you have authority over Dodds?" Paul asked in astonishment.

"Not so. Reverend Dodds selected you for a special role. There's nothing I can do to alter that. His duties are separate from mine."

The bishop eased himself back in his chair and smiled benignly at the wayward pupil.

It took Paul a few moments to grasp the implications of the bishop's words. He could hardly believe what his intellect was telling him.

"We're talking here of a church within the Church – am I right, My Lord Bishop?"

The bishop was disturbed by his comment, Paul could tell. He watched the man squirm uneasily, then quickly recover his practised composure.

"That's an interesting phrase, Reverend Milton. But I'm afraid that it's one – if you chose to use it carelessly – that could cause you much misfortune."

* * *

Paul stormed across the precinct, his emotions swinging between horror and outrage. Dodds had conned him into a situation that was insupportable. And now he had dragged a reluctant bishop into his schemes. He had no-one on his side. He was caught in a no-man's-land between two opposing forces, neither of which he had any allegiance to or whose behaviour he could condone. He had no choice but resign.

But something was stopping him from taking that step. For a moment his mind was a tempest of confusion. Then he realised what was preventing him. It was simple curiosity. He had become unwittingly involved in a world far removed from what passed for normality. And it intrigued him. He wanted to find out more, as long as it wasn't at too great a cost.

As he passed the last building in the precinct on his return to the car park he spotted a plaque by a tall Georgian doorway: *Institute of Advanced Geomantic Studies* and, underneath: *Principal: Julius Dodds.* After Dodds's name there was a long string of qualifications, none of which Paul recognised. Bought doctorates, no doubt, he thought to himself.

On an impulse he knocked on the door. A cold-eyed monk, clad in regulation brown, answered.

"I wish to speak to Reverend Dodds," Paul announced solemnly.

"You are?" the monk asked.

"Paul Milton."

"You have an appointment?"

"Course not," Paul retorted angrily. "I work for him."

"I'm afraid, without an appointment, it won't be possible to speak to anyone," the monk replied coolly.

"We'll see about that!"

Paul stepped forward briskly, with the intention of forcing his way past the monk. As he sprang up the steps and pushed his way inside two menacing monks emerged from the shadows of a small lobby and blocked his advance. He backed off.

"Make an appointment," the cold-eyed monk advised.

"Okay," Paul assented. "I'll make one now."

"I regret I can only make appointments via email or telephone," the monk insisted. "And only if the caller is an approved associate."

Paul took out his mobile. "NOW!! I'm an employee!"

The two menacing monks took Paul's arms and hurled him from the building. He was on his feet again in a moment and half way up the steps when the cold-eyed monk shut the door in his face.

Reverend Dodds looked down on the scene from a first-floor window.

* * *

Paul approached the enquiry desk in the city library. The female library assistant looked up from a desk covered in official papers.

"I want something on the Celts," he announced. "Really arcane stuff. Probably something on Celtic magic."

The library assistant gave him an odd look. He realised that he was still wearing his clerical collar and had not thought to remove it. He followed her to a set of shelves in the non-fiction section, that were identified as *British History/Folklore.* There were many gaps on the shelves, with no books at all.

"Oh my goodness!" she exclaimed. "Someone seems to have taken all the books on folklore! You'll have to request one."

"I don't know precise titles, so perhaps you can ring me when some folklore books are returned and I'll come in and look at them," he suggested.

He gave her his address and phone number and she typed them on the computer.

"Low Moor vicarage," she smiled in apparent recognition. "That's near Walden. It's a beautiful area. But you've got to be careful on those moors."

"Why is that?" he asked, with immediate curiosity. "I've only just arrived and I know nothing about the area."

"Strange things have happened on those moors," she replied mysteriously. "Why don't you see what you can find on one of our computers."

He paid for an hour and sat with other readers at a row of computers. He searched for *Walden, parish of, North of England.* No sooner had he clicked on the search button than his computer burst into flames. All the other computers blew, one by one, right along the row. Readers panicked and fled. He stared at the mayhem in disbelief.

He left the library and went into a gents' outfitters. He came out a few minutes later wearing a trendy scarf over his clerical collar.

He stopped outside the city's occult shop. The building had *CHAOS* written in large black and red capitals across the wall above the doorway.

The capital letters dripped with fake blood. The windows and door were heavily secured. He pressed the intercom. A voice came tinnily back to him.

"What?"

"I need a book on Celtic magic," he told the voice.

"Great," the voice replied. "You've come to the right place."

He heard the sound of the security door being electronically released. He found himself in a large room packed with books from floor to ceiling: works on traditional ritual magic, chaos magic, The Golden Dawn, witchcraft, the Kabbalah, UFOs, the paranormal and booklets on Tarot, ley hunting, sacred geometry and OOBEs. There was an entire six-shelf section dedicated to folklore. He wondered if this was where the library books had ended up.

He waited at the counter. The occult shop assistant, a gigantic Goth, approached with a book entitled *Ancient Rites of the Pagan Celts.*

"Fucking amazing stuff in here, mate! Won't find this in academic libraries."

Paul smiled widely. "That's what I want to hear."

He paid and the Goth wrapped the book in plain brown paper.

"Why all the security?" Paul asked, feigning ignorance.

"Christians," the Goth informed him with a scowl. "They'd like to close us down. Those brown-robed monks are the worst. Fucking fanatics! Tried to firebomb us a month back. Had to repaint the front wall."

Paul left with his anonymous brown parcel. He was relieved he'd had the presence of mind to cover his clerical collar.

* * *

He approached the offices of *The Northern Gazette.* He peered in the window, walked past, then turned quickly down a side alley.

He was pleased there seemed to be no surveillance cameras anywhere nearby.

The first door he came to was locked, but the second gave to his touch and he hurried straight into the back offices of the newspaper.

He ran up a staircase, paced rapidly along first floor corridors, glancing into rooms where staff worked busily. At last he found an empty office with a computer on a desk. The computer was switched on. He slipped quickly into the room.

He sat at the computer and typed in *Walden Moor.* When he clicked *Search* pages showing newspaper articles came up on the screen. He scrolled through them, reading odd sentences that grabbed his attention. Headlines screamed: *MYSTERY OF WOMAN'S DISAPPEARANCE. NO TRACE OF WOMAN LOST ON MOORS. SEARCH CALLED OFF FOR MISSING WOMAN.*

He printed off page after page, helped himself to a document wallet and put the printed pages inside. He had just finished printing the last page when the computer burst into flames.

"Too late!" he exclaimed with a savage laugh.

As he turned from the alley into the street he heard the fire alarm sound.

Chapter Eight

Paul stepped into the nave of All Saints church. Arthur was busy fixing a new pulpit light.

"Arthur," he said sternly, "I need a word."

They sat together in a pew, the *Gazette* articles between them. Paul held up one of the articles.

"Joan Preston vanished in Walden in 1985. She was never found. I discovered her booklet recently."

He held up the *St Martin's* booklet and pointed to the owner's name and the date inside: *Joan Preston. Durham. 1985.*

"I found it hidden in the vicarage study," Paul continued. "How come? Was she having a fling with a vicar?"

Arthur appeared increasingly uncomfortable. He barely seemed able to look at the documents Paul brandished before his eyes.

"Come on, Arthur," Paul insisted. "I want answers!"

"I believe Reverend Reed found the booklet...in St Martin's church." Arthur began hesitantly. "He was the vicar here back then."

"So she went there. Then she vanished." Paul tried to meet Arthur's evasive eyes.

"It seems she did," Arthur managed.

"But she's not the only one, is she?"

Arthur looked apprehensive. He made no reply.

Paul consulted another article. "Esther Parks disappeared in 1944." He read from the article:

"Esther Parks, the widowed mother of an evacuee, was visiting her daughter in Low Moor... She was last seen on 29 September, picking wild flowers in the vicinity of St Martin's church."

He looked at Arthur. "What do you make of that?"

Arthur looked away, obviously troubled. Paul sifted through more articles.

"There's Edmund Reason," Paul continued, "teacher at Low Moor school – and the author of this very booklet – who went missing in 1910." He quoted another article:

"Mr Reason, a middle-aged bachelor, liked walking on the moors. He went out one October day and never returned. A four-day search produced nothing."

He put the article aside. "The loss of Reason...does that make macabre sense to you? Arthur – speak to me!"

Arthur looked down at his hands and muttered in a voice so hushed it was barely audible. "Rumour has it they were all taken."

Paul lowered his own voice out of feigned sympathy for his reluctant companion. "Taken? By whom? For what purpose?"

Arthur looked at his hands. "I can't answer that, Reverend Milton. I hope one day you will find it in you to forgive me."

Paul's anger rose quickly, stung by the man's reluctance. "Can't – or won't answer? Arthur – I need to understand!"

Arthur shook his head. "Whatever I say, it's beyond any man to prove." He looked at Paul, a fearful appeal in his eyes. "I must think of Beryl's safety...and my own." He got to his feet, about to leave. "I'm sorry."

Paul rose too and grabbed Arthur's calloused hands in a spontaneous gesture of support. "Don't fear them, Arthur. Trust in God. Neither Dodds nor Olwen Williams can harm you."

"Can't they?" Arthur replied, pulling his hands away. "You don't know 'em like I do." He stopped speaking abruptly, as if he sensed an immediate, though invisible threat. "I must go now."

With that he was gone from the church.

Paul moved forward to the chancel steps. He knelt and began to pray. "Lord, help me. Show me what I must do."

Images tore at his emotions:

Murdered locals in a potato field, slumped together, as if exhausted from their labours.

The sexually-aroused Olwen, as her younger self, caressing her breasts in a world of mirrors.

The implacable authoritarian Dodds, a man with no human feeling. His monks shooting flying demons and breaking necks.

The sinister heads on the tower arch of St Martin's church, images from another reality that was fraught with spiritual danger.

He was unable to concentrate. He gave up and left the church.

* * *

Paul, his features strained with tension, stepped into the vicarage sitting room. Sarah was making up the fire. She turned to greet him.

"There – look what a fire I've made for you!"

He ignored her comment. "Pack your stuff. We're leaving."

She stared at him in astonishment. "Say again?"

"There's no useful work we can do here," his voice trembled with pent-up emotion. "We've no congregation – and never will have!"

"That's rubbish!" she retorted hotly. "I can go cold calling. Let's do some flyers. I'll take them around Low Moor."

"It's a bit late for that! We've been here a month and you've done next to nothing to help."

They glared furiously at each other.

He's trying to punish me, she thought, because he doesn't want me to have friends. He just wants me to be his personal servant.

She was going to take this badly, he knew, because of her adolescent notions about friendship. But there was nothing he could do to alter that.

He sank into an armchair. He felt the beginnings of a colossal weariness, which would only get worse if they stayed. The cause was an utter dejection of spirit, the result of an obviously futile situation.

"I belong with the poor," he said eventually. "I'll go into social work."

"I can't believe this!" She shook her head. "It's not like you to admit defeat."

"Well, here's a first." His words were like acid flung in her face. "I'm beaten. We're leaving."

* * *

Paul and Sarah sat in the Fiesta, which was loaded with their belongings. He looked determined and focused. She appeared cold and withdrawn. Arthur and Beryl hovered by the car. Arthur clutched a letter.

"I'll give this to Reverend Dodds, as you requested," Arthur said reassuringly.

"Thanks, Arthur." Paul said quietly. "I hope the next vicar proves more amenable than me."

They drove away. Arthur and Beryl, looking distressed, watched them go.

Paul drove fast between the fields beyond Low Moor. The vicarage, All Saints church, the village and the high moorland skylines receded rapidly into the distance. He flung the Fiesta down the road, slammed through the gears on S bends and hills. Sarah suddenly jolted into life.

"I'm not leaving!"

"What?!" He skidded to a stop in the middle of the road.

"I can't," she said simply, but with finality.

"What's the problem? We've no ties here. We can go back to my parents' place until we find something else."

"You don't understand. I feel mum's presence...all around me. Everywhere I go. I can't cut myself off from that."

"It's just wishful thinking. You'll make yourself ill again."

"I tell you – she's here!"

"Well, she'll just have to come with us too!" he growled.

He set off again, determinedly.

"I used to admire you," she said sadly. "You were my hero. You've changed. You've become a coward! Only a coward runs away like this. I thought you were a man of God. You're nothing now."

"They don't want me in Low Moor," he retorted angrily. "You've seen that for yourself. We've had the church open for three Sunday services and no-one came. I thought one or two might have sneaked in at the back simply because they were curious. But they didn't."

"Make them want you! Make them, you coward!" she yelled.

"No! I'll work where I'm needed!"

"We should talk about a divorce!" She lashed him with the words.

"Oh – blackmail!"

"If you want to go – just go! I'm getting out here. I'll walk back."

"Don't be ridiculous!"

"I mean it, Paul. Let me out!"

"SHUT UP!!" he screamed in fury and despair.

He took his attention off the road for a moment and glared at her. The details of his recent life raced before his inner eye, a sequence culminating in the image of a mountaineer swept uncontrollably downhill in an avalanche and heading for a bottomless abyss. He almost cried out with the shock of the vision.

When he turned his eyes back to the road the world had changed. He slammed his foot on the brake as hard as he could. The Fiesta howled to a stop less than a metre from the container of a jack-knifed truck that blocked the entire road.

He stared at the truck. The appalling image of the unstoppable avalanche froze at the edge of the abyss.

He got out and looked in the cab of the truck. It was empty. The driver must have gone to get help. He shouted, but there was no response. He took out his mobile to phone the police but, as usual, there was no signal.

Without a word he turned the car around and headed back towards Low Moor. He felt his face sagging into an expression of weary resignation. There was no escape. He had to accept it.

In the passenger seat, unnoticed by Paul, Sarah smiled triumphantly.

* * *

Back in the vicarage he phoned the police and reported the jack-knifed truck. He was staggered to learn that an officer had passed that very same spot no more than five minutes after him, but had reported no sign of such a vehicle. He was adamant the truck had been there, but to no avail. He rang off.

He called to Sarah, who was unpacking their clothes upstairs. "Sarah, you saw the truck blocking the road, didn't you?"

She appeared on the landing. "What truck? There was a poor injured badger that you had to kill. You said it was an omen."

Chapter Nine

Olwen sat alone by the fire in the basement of her woodland cottage. Candles and the firelight provided the only illumination in the room. The large table stood behind her, with a top of plain scrubbed oak. Heavy old-fashioned cupboards lined the walls. The floor was composed of large stone slabs, worn smooth by many years of feet.

Her sketch of Sarah stood on the mantelpiece. She picked it up and studied it. As if in a fit of absent-mindedness she began to hum a simple melody...

* * *

Sarah was settled on a garden bench at the eastern end of the terrace. Her bike was propped against the house wall behind her. She was glancing at a book on traditional rural crafts, such as thatching, basket weaving and hedge laying. She hummed the same melody as Olwen.

She had a view to her left of the lawn and the churchwarden's cottage. Directly in front of her was the kitchen garden, neatly laid out with rows of vegetables, where Beryl filled her garden basket with potatoes, carrots and the season's first Brussels sprouts.

"Autumn's here and winter's coming," Beryl announced as she scraped the mud from her gardening shoes. "Need to feed your husband up." She put her basket down on the paved path that separated the lawn from the kitchen garden and stepped on to the terrace. "I'd appreciate a hand preparing these, if you could spare a few minutes."

Sarah stopped humming. "Sorry, Beryl. I can't help just now. I have to go out."

Leaving her book on the bench she took her bike and cycled away. Beryl, disappointed and troubled, stared after her.

* * *

Olwen and Sarah walked among the orchard trees of Walden. Two monks observed them from thick undergrowth. Further away, at the edge of the orchard, Gareth and Rhys watched the monks.

"I'm sad you're having problems with your husband," Olwen began, taking Sarah's hand and stroking her long supple fingers. "Men don't understand feminine emotions. It's only mothers who appreciate a daughter's feelings."

She put her arm around Sarah's waist. Sarah rested her head against Olwen's shoulder.

"You're becoming as dear to me as my own mother," Sarah said with a long tremulous sigh. "I'm so glad we found each other."

Olwen smiled sweetly. "It's fate. It was meant to happen."

Sarah turned to Olwen suddenly and looked her full in the eyes. "I feel so free here. As if I haven't any problems. We'll never be parted, will we?"

"Of course not." Olwen smiled reassuringly. "I promise."

They walked away through the orchard trees. Behind them the two monks lay dead in the grass, swiftly and silently garrotted. Gareth and Rhys talked with a group of local men under the trees. The locals carried spades and a light pine stretcher.

* * *

Paul, in clerical collar and dark suit, turned off the A181 and drove slowly through the outskirts of the attractive old city of Durham. He found the address easily and pulled up outside Monica Preston's smart suburban semi. Monica was the younger sister, by a space of two years, of Joan, whose booklet Paul had found in the vicarage study.

He sat in the lounge, where Monica served him coffee and cakes. He felt it was a welcome change from the bishop's unpalatable teabags. Although they had spoken briefly on the phone, when he had taken the opportunity to establish his credentials, as he took a loose-leaf notebook from his briefcase he wondered if he appeared too much like a Church reporter.

Monica's steel-grey hair reminded him too acutely of Julius Dodds but, thankfully, that was as far as any similarities went. She had a kindly and sensitive disposition and thought her answers through carefully before replying to his questions.

"It's very good of you to see me, Miss Preston," he began, shaping his features into what he hoped was a benign vicarly smile. "I don't wish to cause you any distress, but I was wondering if we could talk about your sister's mysterious disappearance?"

"As I said on the phone, there isn't very much I can tell you, Reverend Milton," Monica replied with an apologetic smile. "I hope this won't be a wasted journey for you."

"I'm sure it won't. I'd just be happy if you could tell me anything you feel might be relevant. Any little detail, even if it might seem trivial."

Monica thought for a minute. "It was 1985. I got to hear from the police that Joan was missing – I remember it was the first day of October – when she didn't return to her hotel. There was a local vicar too, a Reverend Reed, who found my phone number. He rang me once to let me know he was doing his best to find her, then I never heard another word from him. I do remember that his manner was a little odd and I wondered if he knew more than he was saying. But I never had the chance to speak with him again. The police didn't have much to say either until, after a couple of weeks, they told me they were calling off the search. I'd put an appeal in all the northern papers, but it made no difference. No-one seemed to have seen her."

"Why was your sister in a hotel?" Paul asked.

"Joan was on holiday. I should have been with her, but I didn't care for those trips of hers."

Her comment set him wondering. "What sort of holidays did your sister take?"

"She liked old buildings, especially churches. She was obsessed with what she called *pagan survivals.* I found it all very spooky."

He scribbled notes as she spoke. He had the clear feeling he was on the edge of a revelation. "What kind of pagan survivals?"

"Forgive me, Reverend Milton, it's not really my subject, but Joan believed most old churches were built on pagan sites. At any rate, the pre-Reformation ones. Sometimes a few pagan bits and pieces still remained. Ancient demons on the corbel table. That kind of thing."

"How did Joan travel around? Did she have a car?"

"Oh no. She used local buses." Monica smiled indulgently at his ignorance. "There were still buses to most places back then."

"She'd look at a church like this, perhaps?" He passed her the *St Martin's* booklet, hoping his timing was not too rushed.

Monica opened the booklet. "Oh – it's Joan's handwriting. Where did – ?"

"It turned up in the vicarage." He didn't feel it wise to go into details.

She dabbed tearful eyes as she turned the pages of her sister's booklet. "Joan was hoping to go to Walden to look at the church. I told the police and they did search the moors. But no-one had seen her arrive. She said the church held a great mystery. Something about it being an ancient gateway. I didn't understand what she meant."

As he was jotting down more notes she handed him a photograph of Joan.

"This is my big sister," Monica said, her voice breaking slightly. "She would have been sixty-nine last month."

Joan Preston, aged thirty-three stared out from the photograph, plain, self-conscious, a little overweight.

"I've had the weirdest feeling all these years," Monica continued, "that Joan stepped through some kind of secret door into a hidden place and couldn't find her way back. It's been truly unbearable to think of."

"What kind of hidden place?" he asked, trying to keep his rush of emotion under control.

"I don't know... Somewhere dark, like a cellar or tomb, but not quite either. Something architectural...like a secret door in a wall. A lost door or doorway Joan found by chance."

He looked at her in horror as she dabbed her eyes again.

* * *

Brown-robed monks with lighted sulphur torches moved warily among the gravestones in All Saints churchyard. Reverend Dodds watched them from the vestry doorway.

Paul strode up angrily. "What's going on here, Dodds?"

"Watch and learn," Reverend Dodds replied icily.

A monk with a flamethrower propelled bursts of flame into the darkest corners of the churchyard. Demons, flushed from their hiding places, fled among the gravestones. Monks with crossbows shot them down. Their companions with burning torches incinerated them. The demons screamed and shrivelled to smouldering rags.

Paul watched in disbelief. A sense of unreality overwhelmed him. He could have been on a film set for a sci-fi movie, but he was in his own churchyard. His mind lurched precariously, as if about to split in two.

"A soul displacer!" Reverend Dodds boomed. "Watch out!"

A soul displacer, more a spiral of shimmering energy than physical substance, moved rapidly through the churchyard. Paul watched as it sprang with manic violence at an old monk, who cried out in alarm. The soul displacer appeared to merge with the old monk's body.

The old monk fell with a cry. The soul displacer seemed to have vanished.

Again Reverend Dodds called out. "It's gained possession! Deal with it!"

The old monk, utterly transformed, rose from the ground snarling and hissing, his features savage and distorted. His gaze fixed on Paul and he launched himself in an attack. Before Paul had realised his danger a demon-hunting monk flung his torch. The old monk burst into flames, emitting ear-splitting screams.

"Oh, God!" Paul cried out in horror and revulsion.

"It's free again!" Reverend Dodds bellowed. "Destroy it!"

The soul displacer ejected itself from the old dying monk. It fled across the churchyard as the monk with the flamethrower intercepted it with a burst of flame.

With a crackling sound like dry leaves consumed in a garden bonfire the soul displacer shrank to flickering blue flame and disappeared.

The hunt for soul displacers continued in the dark corners of the churchyard. Spine-chilling cries filled the night. Paul felt like screaming too, in a futile attempt to banish the new impossible reality that surrounded him.

He stood close to Reverend Dodds by the vestry door. He felt physically safer, but spiritually he was teetering on the edge of that terrible abyss.

Dodds turned to him. "Now you see the evil ranged against us, Reverend Milton."

"What are they?" Paul asked in dismay.

"They are the Devil's army," Dodds stated forcefully, "summoned by the witch of Walden. What you've seen is merely a raiding party. The whole force is massing in the Otherworld, awaiting her bidding. They can only be destroyed by fire or sulphur. The soul displacers are the worst. They inhabit graveyards, places of darkness. This is her revenge for what she imagines we've done to her."

"How in God's Name do they displace a soul?" Paul asked, his mind in complete turmoil.

"They take possession through the mouth or navel, any suitable orifice. Then, in their new human forms, they turn on each other. They know only violence. This is how the human race will be destroyed if we do nothing."

As well as demons and soul displacers another matter was weighing on Paul's mind. He decided to tackle Dodds on the subject.

"I've been trying to find information on Walden, but all the computers I use burst into flames. Why is this happening?"

"That sorceress has cast a protective shield – an occult firewall if you will – around the parish of Walden. Only the chosen can pass through it. If others try they are quickly removed. Technical gadgets like computers are simply consumed by fire if their users try to invade her space."

"Are you able to pass through her firewall?" Paul asked.

"My personal aura is proof against any magic she may try to inflict on me," Reverend Dodds remarked drily. "The only reason you and your wife can go there is because she lets you."

He went to the charred body of the old dead monk and shone an optical lamp into his eyes. "His soul still has contact." He pressed his cross on the dead monk's forehead. "May God readmit you into His Holy Church," he intoned solemnly. Then, turning to Paul: "He will rejoin us in spirit."

Their work finished for the present, the monks made their way from the churchyard, taking their dead brother with them.

"Be careful walking home, Reverend Milton," Dodds remarked as he too turned to leave. "The world is not what it used to be."

* * *

The next morning, when Paul had struggled to force a light breakfast into his reluctant stomach, he returned to the main bedroom for the book of prayers he had left on his bedside table. Reading the prayers was the only way he could quieten his mind and sleep. When he walked into the room he found Beryl polishing the furniture.

"You really don't need to do this, Beryl," he said. "A bit of cleaning isn't beneath either Sarah or myself."

"I've cleaned this place for over thirty years," she replied with a smile. "Don't see why I should stop now. For the last hundred years and more the vicars here have had churchwardens-cum-general factotums."

"But I've no congregation," he replied with a laugh. "I can clean all day long if I wish."

"Things can get pretty hectic here at times," she resumed polishing as she spoke, "and you'll need every hour that comes."

"Hectic? I don't understand."

"You will," she replied enigmatically. "And then you'll be glad we're around!"

He didn't probe further, feeling it was simpler to take her at her word and wait for the new *hectic* circumstances to arrive. He pointed to the four-poster bed.

"Strange thing to find in a vicarage, isn't it? Do you know how it got here?"

She paused in her cleaning and stared at the bed, as if she was seeing it properly for the first time. "I've never really thought about it before, but I suppose you could say it's a bit odd," she admitted. "Reverend West had it made, back in 1990. A firm from away designed it specially. Even came here to fix it up."

"Why would a single vicar want something like this?" he said, puzzled. He was about to ask if West was sleeping with the local wenches, but thought his joke might not be appreciated.

"No idea," she shrugged. "But he said he couldn't sleep easy without it."

When she had gone he hurried to the door and locked it. His attention centred on the four-poster bed. An hour later he had the bed in pieces. He discovered that one of the canopy supports was hollow. Within it he found a long document tube, which he examined in the light from the window. The document tube bore no identifying marks. He opened the top of the tube and peered inside, hoping the tube wasn't empty. He was not disappointed. The tube contained what looked like a rolled document.

He reassembled the bed, then took the tube into the study. He opened it and withdrew two documents, one rolled inside the other. He spread them out carefully on the desk, holding the corners down beneath heavy paperweights.

The first document was a copy of an Ordnance Survey large-scale map of the local area. The second was some kind of plan drawn on tracing paper. It showed a pattern of eight lines, in the shape of a slightly irregular double X, that radiated from a central point, which was marked by a shaded rectangle.

When he laid the tracing paper plan on top of the large-scale map he found that the central point indicated by the rectangle fitted perfectly over St Martin's church. He followed one of the superimposed lines with his finger, looking through the tracing paper to the sites on the map beneath. He realised that the line was actually two lines, or one continuous line, with the church at the centre.

He read off the sites: "Tumulus. Standing stone. St Martin's church. Cailleach's well. All Saints church. Moortop cairn." He stood back from the desk and stared at the documents in astonishment. "A geomantic plan!" he exclaimed. "So that's the secret they're fighting for!"

Sarah appeared in the doorway. He rolled up the documents quickly.

"What are you doing?" she asked.

"Nothing in particular," he replied evasively.

"What have you got there?" she persisted.

"It wouldn't interest you."

"Try me."

"Spying, aren't you? For that Olwen Williams?" he said accusingly.

"What rubbish you talk these days!"

She left huffily. He returned the documents to the tube and hid it under the loose floorboard in the dark space where he had found Joan Preston's booklet.

* * *

Paul sat by the fire in the vicarage sitting room reading *Ancient Rites of the Pagan Celts*. The hands of the wall clock moved around from 1 p.m. to 5 p.m. Unwashed cups and cake crumbs littered the coffee table.

He made the following comments in his notebook, summarising pages from *Pagan Celts*:

A Gatekeeper is a prisoner, a psychic slave.

A channel for spirits to pass between the worlds. A kind of Otherworld guardian figure, like Tam Lin, held captive by powerful magic in a specific geographical location.

The Gatekeeper is known as THE CONDUIT OF SOULS or simply THE CHANNEL. The Celts in the past used prisoners of war to fulfil this role.

He stared at his notes. "A gateway needs a Gatekeeper. But there are no prisoners of war today. Oh, God! It's monstrous!"

He grabbed his jacket and rushed from the house. There was just enough daylight left for him to confirm his suspicions.

Driving fast towards Walden he passed two dead locals, their foreheads branded with a cross, lying at the side of the lane. His emotions barely flickered as he drove by, so unlike the first time, when he had found the two dead potato growers. He was astonished by the extent to which he had changed.

As usual he parked half a mile from the church, at one side of the T-junction, where he could more easily turn the Fiesta around. He jogged up the narrow lane and entered the churchyard. There was no sign of Olwen or her easel.

He went straight into the twilit church and stood beneath the carved heads on the tower arch. He focused on the Giant, letting his perception rush into the gaping mouth. The centrifuge of energy swirled furiously, but this time he willed himself to hang on.

The vibration came to him again...the pulsing of a heart. Then the swirling seemed to slow down and an image appeared, fleetingly, emerging from a misty darkness...

A human face, a little distorted, but recognisable...

"Oh, God!" he thought, in an agony of horror and despair. "Joan Preston!"

* * *

Paul, dressed formally, strode into Dodds's office. He had made the appointment by phone, but gained the impression from the monk on the other end that he was already expected. Reverend Dodds sat at his desk, his ebony staff with its sunwheel symbol lay before him. The symbol reminded Paul of the geomantic plan he had discovered in the four-poster bed, but he decided not to mention it until he had more evidence.

Dodds motioned him to a chair. "You've made more discoveries, Reverend Milton."

There was a note of sarcasm in the man's tone that Paul did not care for. He remained standing. Had Dodds's thugs been spying on him as he rushed into St Martin's church and made his shattering discovery? Had he any private life left? He threw his notebook on the desk. Dodds picked it up and glanced at Paul's notes.

"Joan Preston. Esther Parks. Edmund Reason. Am I supposed to know these people?"

"You amaze me, Dodds!" Paul exploded. "You sit there and lie like a politician! Which proves to me that's what you really are!"

"Please sit," Reverend Dodds replied acidly. "Be civilised."

Paul remained standing. Reverend Dodds pulled his staff a little closer.

"Why didn't you tell me St Martin's is an Otherworld gateway?" Paul asked angrily.

"You wouldn't have believed me. You had to find out for yourself."

"It's spiritual murder!"

"Indeed it is," Dodds agreed. He raised his staff and pointed it at Paul. "Please sit."

Paul felt a vibration pass through him from the staff like a mild electric shock. He felt the power of Dodds's will working on him, using the staff like a weapon. Fighting the man was pointless. He took the offered chair at last.

"To keep the gateway open," Reverend Dodds continued, "a living being must be taken. A Gatekeeper."

"Like Tam Lin?"

"Precisely."

"Just what exactly is meant by the term *Conduit of Souls*?" Paul asked.

"It means quite simply a channel of living energy, through which adepts pass between the worlds. I stress *adepts.* Preparation for the translocation is necessarily rigorous. Another term for a Gatekeeper is a Guardian, who challenges those who are forbidden access, who are not worthy or are not yet ready. You will have come across many Guardians in your reading of folklore." Dodds fixed Paul with his chilling gaze. "But times have changed. In future the gateway will be used to let in the Devil's army!"

Doubt and suspicion filled Paul's features. "How do I know you didn't stage-manage that entire business in All Saints churchyard?"

"What would have been the point?" Dodds replied with the hint of a mocking sneer.

"To make me afraid. A man driven by fear will do as he's told."

"Those demons came through the gateway. Believe me."

"And how will Olwen Williams get them back?" Paul asked sceptically.

"She won't, not until they have fulfilled their purpose," Dodds replied. "Once she's used them to destroy her opponents, which includes at the very least myself and members of the Church, they'll turn on each other. That's her master stroke. Hideous but brilliant."

"Why should I believe a politician?" Paul asked, glaring unflinchingly at Reverend Dodds.

"We are at war, Reverend Milton! You've seen it for yourself! Are you going to be my ally?"

Paul pondered. His eyes were drawn to a tall glass-fronted cabinet behind Dodds's desk. The cabinet was filled with document tubes, like the one from the vicarage.

"I'll have to think," he replied.

"Don't take too long." Reverend Dodds's voice betrayed a definite suggestion of urgency. "The ancient festival of All Hallows Eve is approaching. We must prepare and be ready for it."

* * *

The murdered bodies of two monks, impaled by spears to orchard trees, hung limp as badly stuffed dummies. Gareth, Rhys and several male companions melted silently away among the trees.

Sarah cycled past, but didn't spot the grim remains. Olwen appeared some way ahead, carrying a large wicker basket. She waved to Sarah.

"Sarah, come and collect herbs with me!"

Sarah propped her bicycle against a tree and followed Olwen through a damson orchard.

"What are we looking for?" Sarah asked.

"Valerian and fumitory," Olwen replied. "Valerian to reduce stress and induce sleep. And fumitory is something I always need at this time of the year to use in our seasonal celebrations. We must collect only the roots of valerian and the leaves and seeds of fumitory."

"How wonderful to have such knowledge!" Sarah exclaimed. "Just to look at a hedgerow or walk through a wood and see all the helpful plants growing there."

Olwen nodded gravely. "All healing comes from nature, in one way or another."

They found valerian growing in an old wall at the end of the orchard. The roots were impossible to find among the stones, but the plants at the foot of the wall were easier to dig up. Sarah dug out the roots with a small wooden trowel Olwen produced from her basket. When Olwen decided she had enough they moved on to look for fumitory.

They found the shrubs on open ground between the orchard and a field of vegetables. As they were finishing their collection of fumitory leaves Sarah heard laughter coming from the orchard behind them...

Paul, meanwhile, drove slowly through the lanes of Walden. He noticed the dead monks, but drove determinedly on, his anxiety increasing. Several times he stopped the car and got out, peering into the laneside orchards.

"Sarah?" he called. "SARAH!?"

He got no reply except the cackling laughter of green woodpeckers.

Eventually he caught the sound of distant voices drifting through the trees. Leaving his car on the verge, he hurried towards it...

As Paul drew nearer Rhiannon, Gareth, Rhys and Gwenda emerged from the orchard to meet up with Olwen and Sarah.

"Sarah has been helping me with the herbs," Olwen announced. "She has truly earned her place as a member of our special group."

"Well, we'd better have an initiation," Gareth said with a laugh.

"All major initiations have blindfolds," Rhiannon stated. "And so do ours."

They followed Gareth to a clearing in the centre of the orchard where all six of them tied headscarves across their faces to hide their eyes. Olwen tied a spare headscarf on Sarah.

"Don't worry," Olwen said kindly. "Whoever bumps into you will be an equal and a friend. The nature of the initiation is to establish trust. If you accept the friend freely and openly you will have passed the test. Thereafter you will trust us – and we will also trust you."

"Are we all ready?" Gwenda asked. "Then let's begin!"

Sarah felt excited. She had no idea what would happen, but it all seemed such fun. She thought that four people did bump into her. The first was female, with hands that unzipped her summer dress and lips that pressed against hers. At first she wanted to pull back, but the hands played over her naked body so expertly she was quickly aroused. A second female followed and within seconds she was caressing her in return.

Then the men arrived. She couldn't tell if the first one was Gareth or Rhys. But she was so stimulated she didn't care. After that she didn't mind what happened. She seemed to be passed or spun from one to the other, until she sank on to the grass in blissful oblivion.

Olwen took off her blindfold and pulled her to her feet.

"I'm pleased to say you passed the test, Sarah," Olwen lauged. "Welcome to our special group!"

All blindfolds had gone now. They all kissed Sarah gently on her breasts, except Olwen, who kissed her on the forehead...

Paul, shocked, but unable to turn away, watched from the bushes. Several times he wanted to intervene, but he was unable to move forwards or call out, as if the orchard was protected by a magical barrier...

After everyone had kissed Sarah and bid her welcome, Rhys flung out his arms and shouted "Let's dance!"

They grasped each other's hands and danced in a circle as two locals appeared with squeezebox and flute. Everyone seemed to be looking at Sarah and laughing.

Repulsed but mesmerised Paul agonised in the bushes. Suddenly he turned and fled, wretched and ashamed.

Olwen saw him and smiled to herself. Sarah was too busy dancing, oblivious of her husband's presence.

* * *

Paul knelt before the altar in All Saints church. He tried to pray.

"Lord, help me! HELP ME!!" he cried in agony. He attempted to compose himself, but became increasingly distressed. "Lord, why can't I hear you? Why have you abandoned me?"

He gave up his efforts at prayer, got to his feet and turned to leave. Arthur, also at prayer, knelt unobserved in a pew in the nave. He stood up as Paul descended the chancel steps.

Paul was unable to hide his emotional turmoil. Tears filled his eyes, his face was red and swollen with suppressed despair.

Arthur, deeply troubled, stepped in front of him. "You're not well, Reverend Milton."

Paul shook his head, speechless.

"Be with us in the cottage," Arthur offered. "Let us care for you."

Paul seemed completely disoriented. He stumbled slightly and clutched the end of a pew. Arthur took control. He supported Paul and helped him slowly stagger from the church.

Chapter Ten

Paul and Arthur sat by the fireside in the churchwardens' cosy living room. On the table behind them empty plates and serving dishes stood ready to be cleared away. Beryl came in with tea and biscuits.

"Warm yourself, Reverend Milton," she smiled kindly at Paul. "Stay as long as you need."

"You're very understanding, Beryl. I'm grateful to you." Paul felt stronger already, but the shock he had received in Walden still weighed on his spirits like a forwarning of disaster.

Beryl cleared the table and left the men to themselves. Paul warmed his hands at the fire and savoured his expertly-brewed tea.

"You're a truly spiritual man, Reverend Milton. It gladdens my heart." Arthur's voice rang with deep sincerity.

"It's Paul, please," Paul replied. "We're going to be friends and allies now, I hope."

"I believe we are." Arthur rose and took a bound manuscript from a locked cupboard. "I think it's time for you to take a look at this, Paul."

Paul examined the manuscript, which was a record of past incumbents back as far as the late nineteenth century. He turned the pages carefully. There were twelve vicars in all, with himself as the most recent, the thirteenth.

Apart from the dates of duration of the individual incumbencies, none of which were lengthy, there was a significant amount of correspondence between the incumbents and their bishops. Paul skimmed quickly through it. There were carbon copies of letters complaining about the declining congregation at Low Moor and the 'bad atmosphere' in All Saints church. Reverend Dodds's name was mentioned from the mid-1970s onwards, mostly concerning the culture of secrecy that surrounded him and his 'sinister' brown-robed monks.

The name of Olwen Williams occurred occasionally, invariably in connection with her 'dubious activities' and her 'obstructive nature', although the inferences were vague and impersonal. What struck Paul most forcibly was that she appeared to have been around since at least the beginning of the twentieth century.

A major point at issue was the possible deconsecration of St Martin's church. While the bishop saw no reason to keep the ruined building – which had evidently been deteriorating since the incumbency of Thomas Marshall in the 1850s – Reverend Dodds was adamantly opposed to any moves to deconsecrate. It seemed from the correspondence that, so far, Dodds had got his way.

There was information concerning the reasons for the termination of the individual incumbencies, many of which indicated tragic events.

"Why show me this now, Arthur?" Paul asked. "What's changed?"

Arthur shook his head sadly. "You asked me for help. I refused you. I turned away. I felt as if I'd denied Christ. I want to make up for that. But first I want to know if you can forgive me."

"God forgives you," Paul replied. "So how can I do otherwise? Just tell me how you and Beryl came to be here and how you got hold of this manuscript."

Arthur seemed deeply relieved by Paul's generosity of spirit. He eased himself back in his chair. "I'm the last of a line of secret representatives of the bishop's spiritual church," he began. "The idea was set in motion in 1890 as a way to monitor events in Low Moor and Walden."

"You're implying Dodds's church is not spiritual?" Paul asked.

"It's about as spiritual as a crucifixion nail!" Arthur retorted grimly. "We volunteered to come here because of the deteriorating situation in Walden."

"And you found yourselves swallowed up in Dodds's war?"

"Dodds is a liar. He's no better than that sorceress. He wants power. Don't trust him." Arthur warned.

"Does either Olwen Williams or Julius Dodds suspect you?"

"What they see must be what they believe. I'm just a simple churchwarden. I look after the maintenance. The fact that I'm the bishop's agent is an entirely private matter, like my faith. I have to admit I was deeply upset by the decline of poor Reverend Oliver's mental heath. I almost lost my faith then. But now, thanks to you, my faith has been restored. I can sense in you a man of deep spiritual integrity."

"What happened to my predecessors?" As Paul asked the question he felt a twinge of trepidation.

"I've known four," Arthur replied. "Dodds chose them and they all worked for him, spying in Walden. Or, at least, that was what they were supposed to do."

He took the manuscript from Paul and turned to the photograph of Reverend Gilbert Reed.

"Gilbert Reed did his best to hold to his vocation, in spite of Dodds and the sorceress. The events at the end of his incumbency are not contained in the manuscript. But some of 'em he told to me. Because of their disturbing nature I kept 'em to myself. Perhaps the time has come to put this material in the manuscript."

"I agree. You tell me your stories and I'll write them up," Paul said decisively. "I'll keep your name out of it and write it in the first person singular, if you prefer."

"No, Paul," Arthur said firmly. "It's time I had the courage to use my own name. It will be obvious all this comes from me anyway, as I was the one who was always around."

"Fair enough," Paul agreed. He had unstinting respect for Arthur now. It was one thing to face down opponents towards whom you felt no fear. It was another matter entirely to put yourself at risk from people who filled you with absolute terror.

Arthur began his account. "One day in late September 1985 Gilbert Reed had visited St Martin's church to report to the bishop on the building's state of repair. Dodds would have been furious, but he knew nothing about the nature of the visit. During the course of his observations Reed found the *St Martin's* booklet on the floor. He looked inside and saw *Joan Preston. Durham. 1985.* He ran outside, fearing that Joan Preston, whoever she might have been, was about to be taken by the sorceress.

"He caught up with Olwen Williams and her usual entourage on the field path that leads from the church into the woods of Walden. He realised a stranger, who he thought must be Joan Preston, was with them. Olwen and Joan walked arm in arm, as if they'd known each other for years...

"But Gilbert wasn't fooled. He protested that they should let the lady go, but his remonstrations made Olwen furious and she told him to mind his own business. She took a handful of grain from beneath her cloak and cast it at him. The grain became a swarm of bees that attacked him and sent him fleeing back to St Martin's church.

"He tried to get Dodds to intervene, but the man would have none of it. He realised that Julius Dodds had no compassion and placed no value on human life. Dodds told Gilbert Reed to do nothing...

"But he couldn't. Reed set off to Olwen Williams's cottage to demand Joan's release. He obviously failed, because the next day Dodds found him hanging from a yew tree near the church and had those monks of his cut him down. The matter was hushed up to avoid a scandal."

Paul stopped Arthur's narrative with a question: "So you knew Joan Preston had been taken for a Gatekeeper?"

"I know nothing about Gatekeepers," Arthur replied. "I thought she might have been taken for a *Samhain* sacrifice."

"Where did that notion come from?" Paul demanded in surprise.

"It's just what some of the locals in Low Moor had said about Esther Parks and Edmund Reason, because they both disappeared a month or so before that ancient festival."

"The festival of *Samhain* that we now call All Hallows and All Saints?"

"That's right. The sorceress accused us of stealing it."

"You didn't pursue the Joan Preston business yourself?"

"I could have. But I didn't want to invoke the wrath of the sorceress. She could have taken her revenge on Beryl and I couldn't risk that."

Paul refrained from passing easy judgement on the churchwarden. He was far from sure that he would have acted differently in Arthur's place.

They moved on to Arthur's account of the fate of Reverend James West. It appeared that over the years – specifically 1989 to the year of his death in 1996 – James West caused immense annoyance to Reverend Dodds, as well as to Olwen Williams. Paul felt West must have been a man of considerable inner strength.

Although Paul realised that Arthur was not aware of it, he felt that West must have had some prior geomantic knowledge – or he had acquired it during his incumbency – because he had evidently spent many summer days prowling about in the landscape with a theodolite and a bagful of local maps. Arthur felt the vicar was merely 'a bit of an odd one'.

"I've no idea what he was doing out on those moors, but he had many rows with Dodds, some of which I mentioned in the manuscript. It seemed Dodds had accused Reverend West of 'trespassing on his jurisdiction', whatever that meant. For his part West had accused Dodds of carrying out a 'monstrous subterfuge', but I hadn't a clue what that was about either."

Arthur's remarks suggested to Paul that James West had worked out for himself that St Martin's church was the centre of some kind of local geomantic system. Apparently West also had confrontations with Olwen Williams and had accused her of causing his temporary blindness in order to prevent him from continuing his investigations. This vicar, Paul felt, was a real force!

Arthur continued. "Reverend West had recovered his sight, but within a few months he lay dead with a broken neck at the foot of a moorland cliff. The story, put around by Dodds, was that the poor man had lost his way in the mist returning from a parochial visit. But West had a rule of never leaving the vicarage after dark or in bad weather, no matter what the parochial need.

"He seemed to me to be increasingly fearful during his last year in office," Arthur went on. "He developed a bad stammer and stopped his Sunday sermons. During his last month he never went further than All Saints church. So what he was doing out on the moors in the dark is a complete mystery. My hunch is that he was lured there by that sorceress.

"The incumbency fell vacant for the best part of a year until the eccentric Francis Gore took up the position in 1998. He lasted eleven years and spent a good deal of his time tinkering with his private collection of vintage motors, which he kept in a vacant barn in Low Moor...

"He seemed to have suddenly decided to restore St Martin's church. It may have been an idea suggested by Dodds, but I can't confirm that. Anyway, he had begun work repairing the stonework in the chancel – and was making good progress – until he was found dead one day, having overturned his car while driving through Low Moor on his way to Walden."

"How did he get his tools and materials up to the church," Paul asked. "There's nowhere to turn a vehicle round."

"He carried them," Arthur replied. "He was a strapping fellow was Francis Gore. Six foot three and eighteen stones. He almost came to blows with Dodds one day – it took four of Dodds's thugs to restrain him."

Paul underlined Arthur's comment in the manuscript: Reverend Francis Gore drove into a tree in Low Moor on a clear day on an open road. He was a very experienced driver.The vehicle showed no mechanical faults. At the inquest the coroner's verdict was death by 'misadventure'.

So far one fact stood out in Arthur's narrative: these three vicars were all strong characters, intelligent and principled. For men like them to come to grief in this unholy war made Paul all the more determined to stand up to Dodds and Olwen Williams. He owed it to Reverends Reed, West and Gore. And also to himself.

Paul noted that the incumbency again fell vacant, this time for over two years, until Michael Oliver arrived. Arthur described him as a cultured man, who detested Dodds's philistinism. He appreciated paintings, which made him particularly vulnerable to Olwen Williams's manipulation.

Arthur was reluctant to go into details, but Paul deduced from his inferences that Oliver had to perform a variety of sexual acts in order to earn each one of Olwen's paintings, of which he had a great many. He eventually grew besotted with her and, as her favours became harder to win, descended into 'mental instability'.

"He had not held a service in All Saints church for over a year and began to hate the sound of the church organ," Arthur said. "At the end I think he was more pagan than Christian. I felt I'd no choice but to make the bishop aware. Then Dodds came shortly after and removed him."

Paul gave the newly elaborated manuscript back to Arthur. "That's a good job done, Arthur. Everything's up to date. Now perhaps I could share something with you."

Half an hour later Paul and Arthur bent over Reverend West's geomantic plan, which was laid on top of the large-scale map and spread over the churchwarden's living room table.

"Never seen anything like this before," Arthur admitted. "Dodds would go crazy if he knew you had 'em."

"It shows St Martin's as a geomantic centre. Reverend West's interest in geomancy was probably why he and Dodds fell out. And it may also have been why West died." Breaking necks, Paul knew, was a speciality of Dodds's thugs.

"This explains so much to me," Arthur said. "I understand now why both Dodds and the sorceress want St Martin's church. If you've got the site you control the lines."

"It's all about power," Paul said with an involuntary shudder. "At least that's the way it seems to me now. Perhaps in the past it was different, the energy projected along the lines may have been more benign, but I'm really not sure. I don't think people have changed that much, not over the last millennium anyway."

"The influence from Walden," Arthur said unhappily. "I wouldn't want either Dodds or the sorceress to have that kind of control."

"Sitting like predatory spiders at the centre of their webs," Paul mused. "It's a chilling thought."

He rolled up the map and plan and returned them to the document tube. "I'd be grateful if you'd lock this away with the manuscript," he said. "The vicarage doesn't seem like a secure home to me at the moment."

Beryl arrived with supper on a tray. "You will stay the night, won't you, Paul?" she asked with a compassionate smile. "I must keep an eye on your health."

Paul accepted graciously.

"Have you any plans for tomorrow, Paul?" Arthur asked.

"You don't happen to have James West's theodolite, by any chance? Or did Dodds confiscate it?"

"I have it stored upstairs," Arthur informed him.

Paul smiled. "I think I'd like to check out James West's mapwork."

Chapter Eleven

Paul, in walking gear, crossed the high moorland above the woods of Walden. He carried a map, binoculars and the theodolite. Half a mile behind him was a standing stone and, half a mile beyond that, the dark moortop mound of a tumulus. Ahead of him lay St Martin's church at the edge of the moor above Walden.

He checked the theodolite, making certain that the tumulus, stone and church were in line. "Perfect."

Eight years earlier, straight after university and before he entered the church, he had begun a career as a trainee surveyor. The career had been short-lived, but it had lasted long enough for him to gain experience on large-scale civil engineering projects and mapping in complex landscapes. Plotting a straight line over open moorland was simple in comparison, as long as the weather was fair and visibility good.

He was enjoying himself. This was a welcome change from Olwen's scheming and Dodds's churchyard skirmishes. But, as he looked at the great sweep of tranquil moorland around him, he realised how deceptive appearances were. This was a dangerous place and he could not afford a moment's complacency. He was in no doubt that his presence had been noted in Walden.

As Paul headed in the direction of St Martin's church Reverend Dodds ascended the moortop tumulus. He watched Paul through binoculars, his features stony and grim. Two monks stood patiently at his side.

"How can Paul Milton know about this?" Dodds fumed. "It's not common knowledge!" He turned to the two monks. "Follow him. Report back."

The monks set off obediently across the moor towards St Martin's church.

* * *

Paul left St Martin's churchyard and followed a path across a sloping pasture towards the dense woodland of Walden. When he reached the edge of the trees he checked his position in relation to the church, although the standing stone and tumulus had now disappeared from view. He consulted his map. He was at the precise point where both the footpath and the alignment entered the woodland.

He had a nagging feeling that someone was watching him. He wondered if he was becoming paranoid, but the feeling persisted in spite of his rational doubts.

He waited within the cover of the trees, his binoculars trained on the church and churchyard wall. But he saw no signs of movement. No figures appeared on the footpath between the churchyard and the woods...

Hidden by the churchyard wall the two monks lay in the grass close to the cross base in the corner of St Martin's churchyard. They had removed a stone from the dry-stone wall and peered through the gap.

"He's going on to *her* home ground. If we follow him they'll kill us." One of the monks observed. "She's letting him in. But we won't stand a chance."

"I'll text JD." His companion took out his mobile. "He'll have to get other brothers to pick up the trail in Low Moor."

He began composing his message, while his companion continued peering through the gap in the dry-stone wall...

Unable to find any sign of watchers Paul made his way through the trees. Almost immediately he entered a clearing. A holy well stood on one side, where water flowed into a stone trough from a channel above.

Hawthorn trees, festooned with rags and ribbons, stood above the well. The front of the trough bore the carved words *Old Wife's Well.* He parted the bushes at the side of the well, then stepped back in surprise.

"My God!" he exclaimed under his breath.

A bizarre figure sat among the branches: a larger-than-lifesize effigy, made of interwoven branches and twigs, the body cavity filled with leaves, couch grass and dried moss. It leaned slightly forwards, as if about to stand up.

From his reading of *Ancient Rites of the Pagan Celts* he realised he was looking at the Old Wife herself, the Cailleach of the *Cailleach's Well.* He also knew that this figure was the archetypal Crone of *Samhain,* the ancient Celtic festival marking the beginning of winter and the end of the old year.

He wondered what the Walden festival would be like and how the effigy would be used. As he stared at the figure he had the uncanny feeling he would soon be meeting it again.

He followed the path deeper into the trees. It seemed to follow the alignment: a trackway about ten feet wide cut clean through the middle of the woodland. An attractive old cottage appeared to one side, tucked among giant oaks. He approached cautiously. The sound of voices alerted him and he ducked quickly into cover.

Olwen appeared, accompanied by Rhiannon, Gareth, Rhys and Gwenda. They each carried a pitcher of water and followed the path that led from the holy well. As they entered the cottage Olwen put down her pitcher and turned around. She looked straight at Paul's hiding place. She morphed into her younger self, unfastening her blouse and exposing her breasts.

Paul, in the bushes, stared at her mesmerised.

A couple of hours later he stood by the terminal cairn on the horizon beyond Low Moor. From here he could see most of the sites on the line. The holy well was hidden among the trees, but All Saints church in Low Moor and the other points beyond the Walden woods were in perfect alignment.

He failed to notice two monks lying in deep heather observing him.

* * *

Beryl picked flowers in the vicarage garden. Sarah, wearing a thick cardigan over her summer dress, wafted dreamily towards her.

"Beryl, what are you doing?" she asked with polite disinterest.

"I thought you could put these last chrysanthemums around the house to cheer it up," Beryl suggested. "The rooms would benefit from a bit of colour in these darkening days."

"That's sweet of you," Sarah replied. "Please arrange them wherever you think is best. I just have to go out."

Ten minutes later Sarah cycled away towards Walden. Beryl stood in the back yard gateway staring after her in concern.

Shortly before midday Olwen and Sarah walked together through the Walden orchards, Olwen pointing out different herbs while Sarah wrote descriptions in a notebook.

"Ideally we should have started doing this in spring," Olwen observed, "when the plants are beginning to come back to life. But even late in the year there's still quite a lot to see."

Rhiannon and Gwenda arrived with a basket of food for a picnic. They spread a cloth on the ground and sat around it. Gwenda took bread, cheese and fruit from the basket. Gareth and Rhys arrived with flagons of cider.

"Everything you will eat here was produced in Walden," Rhiannon said proudly to Sarah.

"Even the cider?" Sarah asked.

"Especially the cider!" Rhys laughed. "We've been making cider here since before the Romans came!"

On an area of elevated ground half a mile away Reverend Dodds watched them through his binoculars. After a while he lowered the binoculars and smiled with grim satisfaction.

* * *

A little after midnight Paul dodged quickly through the shadows at the rear of Dodds's Institute in the Cathedral precinct. He was dressed in balaclava, tracksuit and trainers and felt as conspicuous as a ten-foot-high neon sign.

He hadn't spotted any surveillance cameras but, to a novice burglar's inexperienced eyes, that didn't mean there were none.

He was in good physical shape and it wasn't too difficult to haul himself up an old-fashioned cast-iron drainpipe and push open an unlocked first-floor sash window. Once inside he found his way to Dodds's office by the light of a small torch. Putting on surgical gloves he opened the glass-fronted cabinet that contained the document tubes.

He took out several tubes and opened them. Each contained a geomantic plan of more accomplished draughtsmanship than the one from the vicarage. He studied them one by one in the light of a desk lamp.

"Salisbury. Exeter. Ely. Lincoln." He opened more tubes. "Durham. Ripon. York. My God – the whole of England!"

He stood back and stared at the plans on the desk as the implication hit him. In the wrong hands this could be the end of democracy, the end of free speech – which was pretty much the same thing – the end ultimately of independent thought.

How close were we to that day? If these plans fell into the hands of a fascist regime systematic mind control could quickly begin. Would we even know it was happening?

It had occurred before. In conversations with members of his parent's intellectual circle the subject of the Third Reich and mind control had occasionally come up. The geomantic study of patterns of alignments had been a priority for the Reich, with the aim of controlling the national psyche of the German people. This much was known fact. Could it happen in England? Was any combination of the offices of church and state fit to have this gigantic responsibility?

Lost in his speculations he was taken by surprise when two monks burst into the room and grabbed him. Incensed, he threw them off, filled by a sense of outrage he had never known before. He landed several solid blows, until he had both monks down on the floor.

But he was in the presence of trained killers, with a degree of ruthlessness only professional assassins possessed. The monks got to their feet, stung to cold fury. They closed in and quickly overpowered him. They pummelled him about the head and body, toying with him, enjoying themselves, prolonging his pain. They spun him around, from one to the other, hitting him with clinical precision, just hard enough to keep him staggering and dazed.

At last Paul sank to his knees and one of the monks moved forward to break his neck. At the same moment Reverend Dodds swept into the room.

"Stop!" Dodds roared. "He's mine."

The monks stood back, licking their bleeding knuckles. Dodds turned to them.

"Sort the plans," he commanded. "And put them away. Don't get blood on them!"

The monks began returning the plans to the cabinet as Paul got to his feet. Reverend Dodds pulled out a chair for him and offered him a large white handkerchief. Paul sat, dabbing his injured face, staining the unsullied snowscape of Dodds's handkerchief with blobs and smears of blood.

"I admire your nerve," Dodds began, his eyes glinting with fierce delight. "Is there anything you wouldn't try to do if you were sufficiently morally motivated?"

"Don't talk to me about morals!" Paul rasped at him. "Power and control – it's what you're both after, you and that sorceress! You want St Martin's because it's a geomantic centre."

"Well, you've seen the ancient networks," Dodds spoke calmly. "It's a rare privilege outside my Order."

"*Ancient* networks?" Paul queried. "How ancient?"

"Very ancient indeed," Dodds replied. "The Christians simply inherited them."

"Don't you mean *stole* them?" Paul responded angrily. "The Christians built churches all over them."

"I can see the witch of Walden has been poisoning your mind. Just because the pagans existed here before the Church arrived, there's no reason to suppose they were any more benign. The opposite may well have been the case, judging by the Druids' predilection for human sacrifice and the Celtic cult of the severed head!" He paused, studying Paul with his penetrating gaze. "All I can truthfully tell you is that most of these alignments were created millennia ago. No-one knows by whom."

"You can't deny that this system is a potential hidden influence," Paul countered. "No-one sees it, but it's there. Whoever controls it runs the country, at least with regard to the system's spiritual influence – which could be evil or benign or any shade between, depending on who's in charge."

"You could put it like that, I suppose." Dodds appeared intrigued by Paul's reasoning.

"Let's just fast-forward this by a few years," Paul suggested. "Let's suppose we have a heavily politicised church – with you and your tame killers supporting it in the background. On the other side we have Olwen Williams and her demons. Some choice!"

"I agree. This system in the wrong hands would be disastrous!"

"And yours are the right ones?"

"It's my duty to safeguard the system," Dodds stated quietly. "And, where I can, to enhance it."

"Who do you work for, Dodds?" Paul flung his words in the man's face. "Who pulls your strings?"

"I'm afraid I'm not at liberty to say – not even to you," Dodds replied acidly.

"You're admitting you work for a secret order," Paul countered.

"I'm admitting nothing. Just let's say we have the wellbeing of this country as our pre-eminent concern. The alternative is chaos and decay. Is that what you want?"

"Of course not," Paul replied. "But I'm curious to know how you think society's disintegration might come about. From communists perhaps? From the most radical elements within the anarchist movement? From a nationalist pro-fascist movement?"

Reverend Dodds fixed Paul with a fearsome withering look. "Some of these groups may well present problems, but they can be readily monitored. However, we have a more urgent imminent threat. Soul displacers are already among us. You've seen first-hand evidence of this. We must work together to save Christian England. Let me present to you a futuristic scenario."

Paul listened as Dodds leaned forward across his desk, conjuring up images that would not have been out of place in a dystopian sci-fi film. The villages of England were in utter ruins, roofless houses, church towers fallen. An ominous yellow twilight was omnipresent. Soul displacers swooped on fleeing human victims – both young and old – then, in their newly acquired physical forms, attacked and destroyed each other. Ghouls ate corpses on the village greens and in the lanes. A few opportunist demons wandered the landscape, hideous and ferocious. The chaos and destruction in the cities was beyond imagination.

"If we fail to act now," Dodds concluded, "England as we know it will be gone within a few years."

"You know, Dodds, you could always get a Hollywood agent with a storyline like that! I'm sure one of their action heroes would be glad to save li'l ole England!" Paul couldn't resist the gibe.

"Your flippancy does you no credit, Reverend Milton," Dodds said drily. "I've shown you the future and it's not very pretty. Work with me and save democracy."

"Democracy?!" Paul exclaimed in outraged astonishment. "Why is it that I don't believe you?"

Chapter Twelve

Paul, his face swollen and bruised from the night's confrontation, strode into the vicarage sitting room. He carried a letter, which he placed on the coffee table with a gesture of finality. Letters, he felt, were absolute and incontrovertible, compared with the transient superficiality of emails. He would ask Beryl to post it. Job done.

Sarah walked in, still in her robe. She went to the window and stared out at the garden, her features transformed by a secret smile.

"Shouldn't you be dressed? It's the middle of the morning." Paul was horrified to realise that he was starting to despise her.

She turned from the window with a mocking glance. "Dressed? For what occasion? Is the bishop visiting?"

"The bishop will never come here while I'm the vicar," he replied emphatically.

She seemed indifferent to his remark. "What's the letter?"

"My resignation."

She almost flew at him, waving her arms and screaming. "I told you – I'm not leaving! If you force me, I'll fade away and die!"

He yelled at her in exasperation: "We can't stay here. This place is insane! Can't you see Olwen Williams is a predator?!"

"She's shown me more love than you ever have! Your love affair's with God!"

"That's an outrageous lie! You must listen to me, Sarah – for your own good!"

"Listen? To a simpering priest? Do what you like! I'm off to Walden!"

She slammed out of the room.

He caught up with her as she was dressing in the main bedroom.

"Sarah, please –" he was begging now, detesting himself, furious with her – "we must trust each other."

"I've nothing to say to you." Her voice and features were uncharacteristically cold. "You're nobody. An ex-vicar. An empty man."

"I'm your husband. I love you!" He hated that his appeal was so lame.

He tried to embrace her. She fought him off.

"Don't! Don't touch me!"

"What have I done?"

"Nothing. That's the point!"

"You have to understand I've got serious problems. And they are all to do with Walden!"

"There's nothing wrong with Walden! The problems are in your own head!"

To an extent she was right. But how could he explain that each time they tried to make love Olwen Williams was there, in the mirror, enticing, mocking, naked. He couldn't get rid of her – he just didn't have enough personal power to eject her from his life by an act of will.

He felt humiliated and lost, then outrage took hold of him. He flung her down on the bed and forced himself on to her. She fought back.

"No! No! No!"

He ripped off her clothes and had savagely violent sex with her. She responded quickly and they reached orgasm in no time. He stood up and fastened his trousers, dismayed by what he had done.

She turned away from him, shocked by her own response. "I'm going to the police. You raped me!"

"You enjoyed it!" he countered.

"It's too late for you to pretend to be my husband!"

She was angry with herself for giving in to him so easily and tossed out the next line to see how much it would wound him.

"I love someone else."

He was stunned. "You don't mean that!"

"I do! I'm in love and it's beautiful. You wouldn't understand."

"Bitch!" he screamed. "You've betrayed us!"

He picked up a bedside chair as if he would smash it down on her. She sat up on the bed in terror, throwing out her arms to protect herself. He flung the chair aside and ran from the room.

* * *

Paul knelt in prayer before the altar in All Saints church. He knelt for a long time, a kneeling shadow, but prayer was impossible. Sarah was right: he was nothing now, an empty man.

Shame and despair drove him to his feet.

"Lord, I asked you for help. I asked for guidance. I received only silence. Not a sign. Not a moment of insight or peace of mind. Not even a hint of your existence. I will no longer kneel. Show me what I should do as a man upright on my own feet! Show me you are with me. Show me you are here!"

The church was silent. Then he heard Olwen's voice. Just a whisper, but it seemed to fill the building.

"MAKE LOVE TO ME!"

He looked around but could see no-one. Dark fluid appeared on the floor of the chancel, black as blood under the moon. Words began to form from it in large bold capitals:

MAKE LOVE TO ME MAKE LOVE TO ME MAKE LOVE TO ME

Olwen's voice came again. He heard sighs and moans, the sounds of a woman in pre-orgasmic ecstasy.

"FUCK ME, PRIEST! YOU KNOW YOU WANT TO! FUCK ME!!"

"Be gone from God's house!" he yelled. But his voice seemed to have no substance, to be no more than the rasping of insects' wings in some forgotten corner of a dusty attic.

He seized his bible, with the idea of locating an appropriate denunciation, but every page he turned bore a taunting message:

HOW IS YOUR LOVELY WIFE?
SARAH NEVER LOVED YOU
SHE ONLY LOVES ME LOVES ME LOVES ME

He was about to hurl his bible to the floor, but restrained himself. What was really happening? He was standing alone in an empty church...there was only himself – himself at war with himself...

But if this was true how come he saw the face of the sorceress in the chalice, in the water of the font?

Was he projecting it? Or was she?

If this was God's church why was He allowing it to be defiled?

Was the sorceress going to drive him beyond the point reached by Michael Oliver, drive him to an extreme, because he fought back in a battle he would inevitably lose? In the end would he remember his wife...would he remember her name? Would he even remember his own?

Oh, horror of horrors! To watch his mind being dismantled, worse even than being brainwashed by the CIA. To watch in full daylight consciousness as his identity was disconnected, every value, every belief cut away, to be replaced by – what?

He turned around and saw words on every surface – walls, floor, lectern, pews – flickering across the surfaces like some diabolical ticker tape:

FUCK ME FUCK ME FUCK ME FUCK ME

If she could do this in a supposed sacred space – a Christian sacred space – then there was no God.

If this was his own doing he was doomed to degenerate into madness, to end up in an asylum like Michael Oliver...

He cried out at the thought and fled from the church.

As he ran down the churchyard path Olwen's voice pursued him like a gusting wind:

"WE'LL HAVE...SUCH A TIME...YOU AND I! LOVE ME! LOVE ME!! LOVE ME!!!"

He ran to his car, with the idea of driving as far away from this crazy place as he could get. The Fiesta was covered with *FUCK ME FUCK ME FUCK ME.*

He heard Olwen's voice again:

"SARAH HAS SUCH A BEAUTIFUL BODY!"

Her words seemed to echo around him, as if they were bouncing off the churchyard wall and the façade of the vicarage:

"Leave me ALONE!!" he screamed.

Dust blew into his face.

He noticed the lights suddenly come on in the vicarage sitting room. He had to find Sarah. He knew it with a rush of startling clarity. Nothing else mattered now. Somehow they had to become reunified, to grasp what was happening and face it together. If they remained at variance with each other they would be destroyed.

Hurtling into the room he was already calling her name: "Sarah! Sarah!"

There was no sign of her.

"SARAH!!"

He raced up the staircase and into their bedroom. No Sarah. He flung open wardrobes and chests of drawers. Her things had gone.

In one of the spare bedrooms the bed had been made up. The wardrobes were filled with her clothes. He stared at them, feeling dislocated and unmoored, as if he was floating away from warm familiar territory into a hostile alien sea.

Olwen's paintings occupied every wall: dark moorland scenes with swirling grasses and anthropomorphic rocks oozing across the foreground.

He stared at them in revulsion.

He examined the bed. It seemed to have been slept in. On the pillow he found a long black hair. He picked it up and held it against the light...

Was this Olwen's hair from her provocative younger form? Or did it belong to that Gareth, who always seemed to be somewhere around? He couldn't tell. What was undeniable was that the sorceress and her dissembling entourage were doing whatever they pleased with his wife.

This was what caused him the most distress, more than the physical evidence of Sarah's betrayal: they appeared to be achieving their aims with hardly any effort at all. He felt helpless.

He sensed his life and his faith, everything that he thought he had achieved, everything that he imagined he had made of himself – all his skills, his high principles and well-honed intellect – leaking out of him like a ballast of sand from a drifting freighter.

He was lost. He sat down on the edge of the bed and wept.

* * *

Some time later, unkempt and unshaven, he stood at the top of the chancel steps, motionless, as if cast in stone. He was dressed in a surplice and clerical collar. Handel's *Messiah* played loudly from a portable CD player.

Suddenly he began screaming. He screamed until he had no voice left. Then he started to rend his clothing, tearing at himself with desperate strength. He fell down and rolled on the chancel floor, foaming at the mouth...

After a while his seizure subsided and he lay still.

Chapter Thirteen

That evening, when Arthur entered the vestry looking for Paul, he found him curled up in his underwear in a foetal position on the floor. He pulled Paul to his feet and sat him in a chair, covered him with a surplice and brought him a glass of water. He held the glass to help Paul drink.

When he had finished the water Arthur refilled the glass. Bit by bit Paul seemed to be regaining his normal awareness.

"Arthur, my friend, she's a devil!" he blurted hoarsely. "*La Belle Dame Sans Merci!*"

"Take it easy, Paul," Arthur advised. "Drink. Be calm."

Paul drank unaided, but his hands trembled. Arthur helped him stand up.

"Let's get you to the cottage."

They were about to step into the chancel when Arthur pulled back.

"We've got company."

They peered through the vestry doorway into the chancel.

A dozen monks stood before the altar. One by one they began to create a curious soundscape, like the eerie wailing of professional mourners at a wake, until their voices merged in a deep drone.

After a while the drone began to generate lightning-like energy that played around the chancel. Crackling electrostatics accompanied the light display. Thunder-like reports filled the air.

A hazy blue light began to build around the droning monks. Reverend Dodds appeared in the chancel arch facing the altar. He carried his ebony staff. The blue light began to coalesce into a pulsing blue globe that hovered above the altar.

Reverend Dodds, his gaze fixed on the blue light, struck the floor twice with his staff. The drone ceased. He struck the floor three times. The blue light passed through the sanctuary window, leaving the glass intact.

Paul and Arthur watched through the vestry doorway.

"Who *is* Dodds?" Paul whispered.

"A demon from the abyss, for all I know." Arthur growled.

"With his very own private army," Paul added, horrified.

"The sorceress might have met her match this time though," Arthur whispered savagely.

* * *

The blue light, moving rapidly along the alignment, passed above *Old Wife's Well.* The water in the trough boiled and churned. The effigy of the *Cailleach* lurched forwards and emitted an ear-splitting screech.

Olwen rose quickly from her chair by her basement fireside. She took powder from a bowl on the mantelpiece and cast it into the fire. The fire roared and blazed with a greenish hue.

The face of the Green Man from the tower arch in St Martin's church appeared in the flames.

"Defend the gateway!" Olwen cried out. "He's attacking us on the line!"

Moonlight divided the nave of St Martin's church into shafts of light and chasms of shadow. The heads on the tower arch were dark, almost invisible, as if petrified in mid-action by some early sainted Christian magician.

All at once foliage began to sprout from the mouth and ears of the Green Man. It spread rapidly over the carved heads, the Cernunnos, the Giant and the demons, waking them into life. Their eyes and mouths began to glow with pale misty light. Their voices groaned and rumbled like distant thunder.

The foliage continued to spread rapidly until it had covered all the walls of the nave, gripping the stonework with its sinewy tendrils as the walls began to shake and tremble. The globe of blue light appeared and hovered above the tower arch – then exploded in a blinding flash.

Small stones showered down from the tops of the walls. Dust hung in the moonlit air. The building stopped shaking, its structure still intact. Then the foliage slowly withdrew into the ears and mouth of the Green Man. None of the heads on the tower arch had been damaged.

Olwen and Rhiannon, both cloaked, hurried into the nave.

"The gateway is saved!" Rhiannon exclaimed with relief.

"We must lose no time," Olwen asserted. "We must prepare."

A circle of lit candles was arranged beneath the carved heads. Olwen and Rhiannon, both naked, entered the circle. With beckoning gestures they drew the candle flames higher and higher, until they became a circle of writhing salamanders.

The salamanders spun into a whirling dance. Olwen and Rhiannon danced with them, faster and faster, until they lost physical form and became invisible, one with the circle of leaping flames.

The church filled with the light of the hurtling salamanders. Firecast shadows, like prancing goblins, bounded around the walls of the nave.

The circle of flames grew higher, until it formed a column of fire. Olwen and Rhiannon materialised from the flames and stood behind the fiery column facing the tower arch. Gareth, Rhys and Gwenda joined them. They called out with one voice:

"CAST HER OUT!!"

Scooping up streamers of salamander fire they flung them into the mouth of the giant. A sound was heard: the pulsing of a heart. The sound grew louder.

"CAST HER OUT!!"

"CAST HER OUT!!"

The pulsing heart abruptly ceased. At a gesture from Olwen the fire went out. The nave became empty and silent. The moon divided the space once more into shafts of light and chasms of shadow.

On the tower arch the giant's mouth belched yellow flame, as if the half-swallowed naked figure gripped between its teeth was being consumed.

* * *

Paul, washed and shaved, sat at the dining table in the churchwarden's living room. He looked drawn, but was managing to eat a small breakfast. Arthur came in with logs for the newly-lit fire.

"Won't you rest a while longer, Paul?" he asked in concern.

"How can I?" Paul answered. "When I came here I had a life. I had faith. I had a wife. Now I have nothing." He rose from the table. "I have to get them back."

He left the cottage, crossed the lawn and entered the vicarage. He climbed the stairs and tried the door of the spare bedroom, but it was locked.

He tapped on the door. "Sarah? We must talk. It's urgent."

There was no response.

He went into the main bedroom and selected his warmest and most robust outdoors' clothing. He crammed it into a stuffsack and went back downstairs. In the sitting room he took his CD player and a small selection of CDs then left the house.

Returning to the cottage he unpacked the stuffsack and changed his clothes. No point wringing his hands in his dog collar, he thought. It was time to take the fight to his enemies.

Carrying the CD player he crossed the churchyard and went into All Saints church. There was no sign Reverend Dodds had been there. Beryl was busy polishing the woodwork.

He inserted a CD of Gregorian chants into the CD player. As soon as *Veni, creator spiritus,* which he thought was the most appropriate choice, filled the church he felt more at ease. He noticed Beryl staring at him in surprise.

"A refreshing change, don't you think, Beryl?" he felt his smile was almost one of a man of peace. An effective disguise, he thought, for a new man of violence.

"I love them," she replied, tears of joy filling her eyes.

"I want you to do me a favour, Beryl, please."

"Anything to help, Paul. You've only to ask."

"I'd like you to play this CD all day until I come back. It lasts exactly seventy-four minutes and thirty-nine seconds."

The chants would send a message along the alignment: that this particular vicar was not going to give in!

* * *

Paul left the church and drove to a small market town twenty-five miles away. He paid for four hours parking and walked to the parish church in the market square. He sat in a pew at the eastern end of the nave and remained there for three hours. He let the tranquil ambience of the place seep into him until he felt it was drawing his own inner peace from some deep internal spring. He could feel it beginning to rise up into his mind until he was filled with a sense of calm he hadn't known for months.

He wondered if he was there to commune with God or with his own life force. He let the question remain open. Then he left the church, called at a couple of shops, returned to his car and drove back to the vicarage. If he hadn't reconnected with God, he thought, at least he had rediscovered his own inner resolve.

Carrying a crowbar and a spray of the strongest weedkiller he could buy without a licence, he went straight to the spare bedroom and prized the door open. The room was empty. He noticed that Olwen's paintings on the walls seemed to have grown more sinister. The anthropomorphic rocks appeared to be slowly changing into malevolent entities:

Suggestions of demons, half animal, half human. Humans with bird-like heads. Human bodies with monstrous heads. Heads with no bodies, only arms and legs. Reptilian and batlike beings. Humans with toads' heads. All taking shape, as if they were about to ooze from the paintings into the room. These must be William Grove's *vile manifestations* he thought with a shudder.

"I'm not going to waste holy water on you!" he growled at them. "Poisoners require poisoning!"

He proceeded to spray weedkiller on the paintings. The demons writhed and grimaced in agony, emitting shrill cries of pain. As he worked he wondered if this was what it was like for the early Christian missionaries, as they walked the length and breadth of these islands casting out devils. When there were no devils left God was supposed to fill the vacuum. Wasn't He?

But if God was so powerful why did He need a human go-between? Why wasn't he strong enough to brush these demons aside for Himself? Was God just sales talk? Was the real power centred in the priest-magician's esoteric training and knowledge? Although these questions caused him emotional discomfort, intellectually he felt they were long overdue.

When the paintings had been thoroughly obliterated and the demons were dripping into a scummy morass on the floor he felt he had thoroughly grasped their provenance. He saw Olwen in his mind's eye projecting with every brush stroke images and energies from some ancient necromancer's grimoire. Well let the sorceress do her worst. He was ready for battle.

He left the bedroom door wide open, walked out of the vicarage and across the lawn to the churchwarden's cottage.

* * *

After they had eaten an early meal Arthur sat by the doorway of his cottage. Dressed in his old coat and hat he was almost invisible in the deepening late-October twilight. He was watching All Saints church, where a soft yellow light was slowly filling the windows of the chancel.

Paul stepped from the cottage. "What's going on, Arthur?"

"Something very strange is happening."

As they watched, the yellow light grew steadily in intensity.

"I'm going to investigate. Go back in the cottage, Arthur. If Dodds is around it's best you're not seen to be involved."

Paul entered the church warily. Yellow light filled the entire building.

"Hello? Who's there? Reverend Dodds? Hello?"

There was no response. Yellow mist seemed to be forming from the light, swirling from the chancel into the nave. As he walked towards the chancel steps he was aware of a sound, faint at first, then growing louder, like the waves of the sea beating on a distant rocky shore.

"Hello? Dodds? Who's there?"

Still no response. He ascended the chancel steps. The yellow light seemed most intense in front of the altar and the mist was also becoming thicker there. He stepped forward. The yellow mist parted before him. Then he saw the naked body of a woman lying on the floor before the altar.

"My God – Joan Preston!" He peered closer. "Not a day older."

Reverend Dodds ascended the chancel steps. "That's right. The last Gatekeeper."

He joined Paul. They looked down at the body.

"Her life force has been used up," Reverend Dodds announced. "They will have to choose a new Gatekeeper to admit the Devil's army. And they will have to do it soon. All Hallows Eve is imminent, the start of the most important festival of the ancient year. We must be ready."

Paul was not paying attention to Dodds's words. Something unbelievable was happening to the body of Joan Preston.

"God help me! Look!"

Joan Preston's body had begun to age, from thirty-five to fifty, to sixty, to sixty-nine. A soft white mist formed around the body...

The body began to be absorbed into the mist, disappearing gradually, the extremities first, then the facial features started to blur...

Paul took out his cross, stepped forward quickly and pressed the cross to Joan's forehead. To his horror the cross passed through the tissue, as if it was as insubstantial as the mist that was absorbing it.

He felt as if he might throw up. "May Christ readmit you into His Holy Church," he managed through clenched teeth.

Then, as he and Reverend Dodds continued to watch, the mist in the chancel faded and vanished. At the same time the tissues of Joan Preston's body became increasingly attenuated until not a single trace of her remained. It was like something from a Hammer horror, as Dracula's remains vanished among the dust and blown leaves of his castle floor.

"Those witches are building their Otherworld army." Dodds's voice thundered in the empty chancel. "When a new Gatekeeper is in place they will open the gateway for soul displacers by the thousand to enter our world. Believe me now, don't you, Reverend Milton?"

Paul stared at his companion with such a look of furious despair it made the disdainful patriarch blink.

"I am surrounded by murderers!" Paul exclaimed.

Not waiting for Reverend Dodds to reply he strode from the church.

Chapter Fourteen

Next morning Paul walked briskly through the woods of Walden to Olwen's cottage. He knocked firmly on the door. There was no response. He tried the door handle, which yielded. He stepped into the house.

He found himself in an old-fashioned kitchen. A peat fire burned in an old black kitchen range. "Okay, Olwen! Here I am!" he announced with a laugh of grim belligerence. "Are you coming out to play with me today? Or do you only come out when Sarah's around?"

Nothing happened.

He walked through the ground-floor rooms, which were sparsely furnished with heavy old-fashioned furniture.

"Olwen!" he called out. "Where are you?"

Silence.

He found a door which led to a staircase. He set off up the stairs. He walked from room to room on the first floor, the furniture again old dark and heavy. When he looked out of windows he saw trees on all sides, massive oaks, gnarled and menacing. He walked along a corridor towards an open door at the end. The door moved a little and creaked in the draughts of the house.

He entered the room at the end of the corridor cautiously. Against a wall, under dust sheets, he found paintings in a long row. Removing the sheets he began looking at the paintings. The first showed Joan Preston, as she was in 1985, standing among swirling grasses in St

Martin's churchyard. The painting bore the usual signature of Olwen Williams.

"Poor Joan," he said to himself.

He noted the words written by hand on the back of the painting:

The Gatekeeper. The Conduit of Souls.

He looked at the next painting, which showed a slim woman of thirty in early 1940's fashions in the swirling grasses of the churchyard.

"Esther Parks."

The next painting revealed a man in his late thirties in Edwardian garb among the gravestones and swirling grasses.

"And Edmund Reason."

Behind this painting were a dozen more, going back, he guessed by the subjects' changing fashions, to the time of the Reformation. What happened before that was a mystery. He wondered if perhaps the Catholic church in these parts had been more amenable to pagans. In the turbulent years of the middle ages some of the more remote communities might have turned a blind eye to who was using their holy ground and how they were using it. Perhaps in some parts they were more pagan than Christian. The former may have claimed it was their ground first anyway.

On all the paintings, right back to the earliest one, was the unmistakable signature of Olwen Williams. What was she then he wondered – archetype or goddess? Or a living incarnation, like an avatar, of the latter?

He realised none of the paintings bore the names of their unfortunate subjects. Because, of course, they were soon to become dehumanised in order for them to fulfil their hideous destiny.

An easel stood by the window supporting a painting covered by a cloth.

"Who's this?" His mocking tone masked his rising fury. "What defenceless creature have you picked on now?"

He whipped off the cloth. The painting that was revealed showed Sarah in St Martin's churchyard. Olwen's sketch of Sarah was pinned to the back above the words *The Gatekeeper.*

"NO!!" he cried in shock and disbelief. "NO!! NOOOO!!"

He ran headlong from the room.

Sarah cycled in through the gates of the vicarage. Rhiannon, Gareth, Rhys and Gwenda emerged from the bushes and blocked her path. Their menacing manner checked her eager smile. Gareth took hold of her handlebars.

"Sexy Sarah!" he laughed.

"The faithless wife!" Gwenda poked Sarah in the ribs.

"What a coup – a vicar's moo!" Rhiannon smirked.

"Get off the bike," Rhys ordered.

Gareth and Rhys pulled the resisting Sarah from her bicycle.

"No! No! Let me go!" Sarah protested. "I'll tell Olwen!"

Rhiannon and her companions laughed darkly.

Arthur emerged from his cottage and ran towards them across the lawn. "Leave the lady alone! This is private property – get out of here!"

"You should learn better manners, pops," Gareth looked at Arthur with a mocking sneer. He picked up a handful of dust from the ground and tossed it into the air. The dust became a flock of jackdaws that attacked Arthur, trying to peck out his eyes. Arthur flung up his arms to defend himself, but was forced backwards across the lawn. Beryl rushed from the cottage brandishing a sweeping brush. She attempted to fight the birds off, swiping at them with the brush, but the birds turned on her as well.

Rhiannon and her companions laughed and dragged the protesting Sarah away.

"Get Paul, Beryl! Tell him what's happened!" Sarah cried out.

Then she was gone. The jackdaws dematerialised, returning to the dust from which they had been made.

Ten minutes later Paul drove in fast and skidded to a stop. He ran straight into the vicarage and raced upstairs. Bursting into the spare bedroom he flung open the wardrobe. It was empty. All Sarah's things had gone, as if she had never existed.

He stared at the empty wardrobe, his emotions in free fall.

Reverend Dodds appeared in the doorway. "I see you've made a good job of those vile objects," he said, smiling grimly at the defaced paintings. "But they had no real power. Designed to frighten, merely."

"Sarah's been taken!" Paul gasped.

Reverend Dodds showed no emotion. "Then you must prepare for the battle of your life," he said with icy finality.

* * *

A low fire glowed balefully in Olwen's basement. Candles glimmered from mantelpiece and shelves. Olwen sat across from Sarah at the plain oak table. Rhys and Gareth held Sarah firmly by arms and shoulders. Gwenda stirred a cooking pot that hung above the fire. Rhiannon filled a small bowl from the pot and placed it in front of Sarah.

"Drink," Olwen commanded. "You must be purified."

"What are you doing?" Sarah shrieked. "I thought we were friends? I thought you were all my friends!"

"We were lying, dear. Haven't you guessed?" Gareth pulled a mock-tragic face.

"You were so easy, compared to your righteous husband. Destroying him will be tremendous fun." Olwen looked at Sarah with a hint of anticipated triumph. "He's been playing Gregorian chants to annoy me. Of course, sacred chanting began with the pagan priests." She looked at Sarah with contempt. "The Christians stole them too and put in their meaningless pietisms."

"Paul will be looking for me. He'll find me!" Sarah asserted with hollow bravado.

"He won't find you. He's too busy searching for God!"

Everyone laughed at Rhiannon's gibe.

Sarah burst into uncontrollable tears. She knocked the bowl from the table.

"You'll drink it. They all do." Olwen remarked blandly.

Gareth and Rhys took tight hold of Sarah. Rhiannon brought another bowl. Sarah screamed and struggled.

"No! No! Let me go!"

They forced her to drink. After a few seconds she became drowsy. Her eyes closed and she slumped forward on the table.

Olwen laughed. "The valerian and fumitory will prepare her. It's a delightful irony that she collected the herbs herself."

Gareth and Rhys let go of Sarah. Gareth filled glasses of wine from an old stone jar and handed them around.

"Here's to the new Gatekeeper!" Rhys shouted jubilantly.

They drained their glasses. Gareth scooped Sarah up in his arms and carried her from the room.

* * *

Paul came out of the churchwarden's cottage. Arthur, his head bandaged, lingered in the doorway.

"Sorry I couldn't stop 'em, Paul," he stated bitterly. "But they seem able to fashion any magic that suits 'em."

Paul looked at Arthur with concern. "I'm just glad they didn't inflict any serious injury."

As they talked they began to notice a change in the quality of light, a reddening of the air to the north, in the direction of Walden.

"Lord save us! Look at that!" Arthur exclaimed.

"It's dust," Paul said with surprise. "I can feel it on my tongue, like the grit of some hellish sirocco." He looked worried suddenly. "You and Beryl lock yourselves in the house. I'll close up the church."

Red dust swirled thickly in the air as Paul battled across the churchyard against the rising wind. He wrenched open the vestry door, but it took all his strength to force it shut again. He locked the doors, then tried to turn on the lights. But there was nothing. No electricity.

The sullen red glow outside the windows filled the church with an eerie russet twilight. Like the hinterland of hell, Paul thought. Fine red dust penetrated the church, hanging in the air and dulling the colours of the stained glass in the east window.

As he stepped into the chancel he noticed a hazy figure sitting at the organ.

"Identify yourself!" he demanded.

The figure removed itself from the organ and walked swiftly towards him. Suddenly Sarah was flinging herself into his arms.

"Sarah!" he exclaimed. "How did you get here?"

"I escaped," she smiled at him through the red gloom. "Aren't I clever? Why don't you give your brave little wife a kiss?"

He pecked her on the cheek, but she seized his head and forced his lips against hers. Her hair bore the faintest smell of woodsmoke and autumn leaves.

He pushed her violently away. "You would do this in God's house? Indulge your dark arts under His sacred roof? Where's Sarah? What have you done with my wife?"

Olwen in her younger form stood before him. "Still clinging to your hollow god? He will never ever save you! As for your wife, she belongs to me now!"

"You're nothing but a mere trickster!" he snapped back at her. "I command you to release my wife!"

"Forget your wife! She can offer you nothing compared with me! I am the one you really desire. You can't resist me, priest!" She forced him back against a pew and overpowered him, then began to rip off his clothes. "Is there a man in here? Let's see if I can find him!"

He tried to push her away. "You won't take my power!"

She laughed harshly and tore off his shirt and trousers. "Power? You have none. But I'll lend you some of mine – then you can fuck me!"

The force of her will overwhelmed him. He felt like an exhausted swimmer, floundering in a relentless undertow. He realised they were naked and she was shoving him on to the altar, pressing herself against him, forcing him into her...

"Now, little priest, fuck a real woman for a change!"

The church doors flew open. The red dust storm entered the church and raged wildly around them. The dust was in his throat and eyes, choking him, almost blinding him. The stained-glass window above the altar shattered. The font cracked in two. The altar crumbled.

"NOOOOO!!" he yelled.

The massive gilded cross on the wall to one side of the east window broke loose and fell. Just in time Olwen stepped away from Paul, her seduction mere seconds away from consummation. She avoided the falling cross by an inch and fled.

Paul lay on the floor, unconscious, beneath the fallen cross.

Chapter Fifteen

Some time in the middle of the night Paul came round. He got to his feet slowly. He was fully dressed. All the lights in the church were turned on. The dust storm had ceased and everything was back to normal. The cross hung in its place on the wall. The east window, font and altar were intact.

He looked around in amazement. "A miracle," he said to himself. "It's a miracle."

He inspected the church. There was no dust. No sign of a struggle. Nothing to indicate that anything unusual had happened. Had he imagined it? Had it been some kind of crazy sexual fantasy? But he could still catch the scent of woodsmoke and autumn leaves from somewhere. He realised it was coming from his jacket collar.

He went to the vestry and covered his clothes with a surplice. Returning to the sanctuary he stood before the altar. He held up his cross and prayed aloud.

"We pray Thee, O Almighty God, that the spirit of wickedness may have no more power over this Thy servant, but that it may flee away and never return."

He sprinkled holy water about himself, on the floor around his feet and on the altar. He knelt in prayer.

"Father, help me to listen, to understand and to remember…"

The pale light of dawn flushed night from the windows. Paul got to his feet, went into the vestry and turned off the lights. Had God truly saved him, he wondered? Or had his struggle with Olwen triggered a clash of primordial forces that pre-existed the very notion of gods? Had his battle with the sorceress been physical, astral or spiritual? He felt humbled by the limits of his understanding.

But something had saved him. And he did indeed feel that a change had taken place deep within his being. He was calm. He felt inwardly stronger, as if a closed-off part of himself had broken through and was nourishing his life. What new awareness might come bubbling up he had no idea. But whatever the change signified it was welcome.

Its origin, whether external or internal, was a mystery. How little we knew about life, he thought. Whatever the source there should be no rush to judgement.

When he stepped back into the chancel he found Julius Dodds, his ebony staff in his hand, waiting for him.

"I'm glad to see you start work early, Reverend Milton," he intoned sonorously.

"I don't suppose you need sleep, do you, Dodds?" Paul replied. "A little foible us mortals have to bear."

Reverend Dodds ignored the comment. "You're aware the All Hallows Eve ritual will begin in Walden this very night?"

"Of course."

"You'll need help," Reverend Dodds suggested in a voice that was almost friendly.

"Not from you, Dodds."

"Suit yourself."

Reverend Dodds walked from the church. Paul, his features resolute, watched him go.

* * *

Paul, in a warm tracksuit, drove away from the vicarage in the direction of Walden. As he left Low Moor he caught glimpses of St Martin's church, the ruin gauntly visible through gaps in the leafless autumn woodland. The distant moors beyond the church were dark and forbidding.

He drove fast, his thoughts focused on the night ahead of him. As if it had been felled by an invisible woodsman a tree on the verge suddenly toppled into his path. He yelled with surprise and slammed on the brakes.

He was too late. He hit the tree, but seemed to pass straight through it. He got out of the Fiesta and looked around in wonder. There was no sign of the fallen tree, no trace of a sawn-off stump on the verge. He inspected the Fiesta for damage, but found none. He got back in the car, waited till he felt calm again, then drove on more slowly.

If this was one of Olwen Williams's mind games he was up for it, but he was also aware that the forces in Walden would employ any means to outwit him. One of their illusions might suddenly turn out to be real.

An apparently solid stone wall appeared, completely blocking the lane. He yelled again involuntarily and applied the brakes. He hit the wall at little more than walking pace and passed through it.

He continued driving. Suddenly an immense torrent of water raged towards him down the middle of the lane. He had no time to react before the water engulfed him. He couldn't help yelling and shut his eyes for a few seconds.

When he opened them there was no sign of water. He had somehow managed to keep the car on the road and hadn't rolled it in a field. He got out of the Fiesta and leaned against a laneside gate, feeling shaken. After a few minutes he decided to get back in the car and carry on. As he stepped towards the Fiesta it exploded in a fireball, throwing him to the ground.

If he had been a few moments sooner there was no doubt he would have been killed. The sorceress was after him with a vengeance.

* * *

In a small basement room in Olwen's house a single candle burned on top of a chest of drawers. Sarah lay on a simple camp bed, naked, drugged, half asleep. Olwen entered and stared down at her possessively. A moment later she morphed into Paul and touched Sarah's hand, awakening her.

Sarah reached towards him. "Oh, Paul, I've been such a fool. Can you ever forgive me? Can God?"

He sat on the bed and ran his fingers through her hair, then kissed her gently on the forehead. "You're safe now. I'll always be here for you. Lie back and relax."

She lay back. He lowered himself gently on top of her. But something wasn't right. After a few moments she began to resist.

"Does God forgive me, Paul? Do you? It's not you, is it? Get off me!"

She fought back hard against him. After a few moments he gave up and morphed back into Olwen.

Olwen got off the bed. "What a sad stupid little thing you are!" she said, glaring balefully down at her. "Why don't you go back to sleep and dream of your God-besotted husband!"

Olwen swept from the room. But her words gave Sarah hope – and from hope came strength. She realised Paul had not succumbed to Olwen's tricks and blandishments. He was out there, she knew, ready to come to her rescue. Whatever happened she just had to focus on that and hang on.

She had been weak, vain and impressionable, like an adolescent girl. She had let Paul down badly, flung her disloyalty in his face. If she survived this ordeal she would do everything she could to make amends.

She did love him, she realised that clearly now. She wondered what he was doing and if he was in danger. Was he risking his life to save her? The thought overwhelmed her with sadness and guilt and she wept bitter tears of remorse.

Rhiannon, Gareth and Rhys appeared in the room. They stared at their prisoner's tearful face.

"She's still remembering too much," Rhiannon said. "She needs more."

While the men held Sarah down Rhiannon forced her to drink another bowl of the horrible concoction.

Within a few seconds all thoughts of Paul had been left far behind, as she plunged into an abyss of drugged forgetfulness.

* * *

Paul sat by the side of the road, staring at the burned-out shell of his car. It had been a lucky escape. Did Olwen think she had finished him off? What powers of clairvoyance did she possess? Could she see him now, or did she assume he was history? Did she ever commit an error of omission?

An idea was taking shape in his mind that brought a grim smile to his face. Maybe it was his turn to play a trick on the sorceress.

He was about to cross the road and disappear into the woodland beyond, with the idea of reaching Walden undetected, when a demon, part-human, part-reptile, emerged from the trees and flung itself at him, attempting to grab his head in its immense jaws. He wrestled with the creature, but could not match its ferocity.

The demon suddenly stiffened and relaxed its grip. He freed himself from its claws and pushed it away. The demon crashed to the ground, a crossbow bolt embedded in the back of its neck.

Two crossbow-wielding monks emerged from behind a screen of elder bushes. Reverend Dodds accompanied them.

"Accept help now?" Dodds asked. To Paul's chagrin the man seemed amused by his plight.

Dodds offered Paul a knife in a leather sheath. "This blade has been cast in a special solution of sulphur. Go for the eyes or the throat of your enemies, they are usually the weakest points. But any wound is better than none."

Reluctantly Paul accepted the knife. Reverend Dodds handed him a silver cross in a small lead-lined box. Paul took it.

"This also has been treated with a sulphur solution." He stared at Paul with cold intensity. "You know what to do with it."

Finally Reverend Dodds tossed him a black hooded cloak. "This won't make you invisible, but it will help to create anonymity." He offered an ironic smile. "You might feel a bit chilly tonight after the heat of the day."

Paul accepted the cloak in silence, as he had the knife and silver cross. Wearing the cloak he continued his journey on foot. When eventually he looked back he saw that Dodds and the two monks had disappeared.

He was alone now, with all his chances before him, with no longer any reliance on the Christian god and with only his wits as his guide.

Chapter Sixteen

Olwen sat by the basement fire, while Rhiannon bent over the scrying mirror which was laid on the table.

"What do you see?" Olwen asked.

"The priest's burned car. Our people are signalling that there isn't a body inside. They are searching the lane...signalling there is nothing to find."

"He'll come to us later," Olwen said matter-of-factly. "We'll deal with him then. He has no power and poses no threat."

Gareth and Gwenda came in with Sarah, who was dressed in a loose robe. She appeared heavily drugged.

"Sit her down," Olwen commanded.

Olwen sat at one end of the table, while Gareth and Gwenda put Sarah in a chair opposite. Rhiannon removed the scrying mirror and slapped Sarah's face hard, causing her eyes to open wide. Gwenda held Sarah's head so that Olwen could look deeply into her eyes.

"This is your true function: to be a channel between the worlds. A pathway for my Otherworld forces. Do you understand?" Olwen asked sternly.

Sarah's eyes were fixed resistlessly on Olwen. "I understand," she echoed. Her voice was flat and without inflection, like the voice of a robot.

Olwen morphed into her third archetype, the Crone, a stooped and aged hag, with wrinkles and wisps of grey hair, a toothless sunken mouth, yellow skin and ferocious red-rimmed eyes.

"Hold me!" she ordered.

Gareth took hold of Olwen's head. A spirit form, an exact double of the Crone, left Olwen and passed into Sarah.

Sarah screamed in agony.

The spirit form returned and merged with Olwen, who morphed back to her usual form.

"Now you are ready," Olwen announced.

Sarah collapsed face down on the table. Gareth and Gwenda dragged her from the room.

Rhys strode in, his face flushed from exertion. "Our people are out on the moor, preparing to charge the earth currents."

"Let the ritual begin!" Olwen called out.

Olwen, Rhiannon and Rhys hurried from the room.

* * *

A group of black-cloaked and hooded figures assembled on the Walden Moor tumulus. A chant and soft drumming began. After several minutes the group processed across the moorland to the standing stone. The chant and drumming intensified. The group paused at the stone.

The setting sun touched the cairn on the far horizon beyond Low Moor. The chant ceased. The drumming grew softer. A pathway of golden light extended from the cairn through St Martin's church and touched the standing stone. The group parted to allow the pathway of light to pass between them. The stone glowed with light, as if it was illuminated from within.

The chant started up again, softly at first, then swelling. The drumming grew louder. The group circled the stone three times, stamping their feet on the worn circle of earth that surrounded it, then processed slowly towards St Martin's church along the pathway of golden light.

The sunlight extended to touch the tumulus, then it gradually started to recede as the sun began to sink.

A second group of cloaked and hooded figures stood in silent meditation around *Old Wife's Well*.

A drum beat softly. The effigy of the *Cailleach*, dressed in cloak and hood, was seated on a litter.

The soft drumming grew louder. The group stamped their feet on the woodland floor and began a stark and simple call-and-response routine. They raised the effigy shoulder high on the litter.

The sun set behind the cairn. The group on Walden Moor processed towards St Martin's church carrying lighted lanterns. The chant began to build, becoming increasingly intense.

The group arrived at St Martin's church and spread out around the churchyard, like defenders of the temenos. A call-and-response routine began.

The rising full moon appeared above the Walden Moor tumulus as if it had risen from the earth. A pathway of silver light extended to the standing stone and on across the moorland to St Martin's church. The pathway spread further, until it touched the cairn on the horizon beyond Low Moor.

The woodland group moved on to stand before Olwen's house, bearing the effigy on its litter. The members of the group stamped their feet and chanted to a simple repetitive drum rhythm.

Sarah, a stumbling figure in a dark hooded cloak, emerged from the house. Olwen, in cloak and hood followed her. She held Sarah on a rope. Rhiannon and Gwenda came next, then Gareth and Rhys, all wearing hooded cloaks.

As Olwen stepped from the house the pathway of silver moonlight touched her. She morphed momentarily into a goddess-like figure with a shimmering silver aura. There was an ecstatic sigh from the group.

Olwen, standing behind Sarah and taking hold of her shoulders, called out: "Behold!Our new Gatekeeper!"

A shout went up, accompanied by vigorous stamping and drumming.

The group processed through the woods, four hooded figures carrying the effigy on its litter. Except for the two drummers everyone carried lighted lanterns. Sarah was urged on with sharp tugs of the rope.

The drumming continued, muffled and fast. Shadows writhed and swirled in the light of the lanterns. Trees by the path shook as if in a storm wind.

The group paused to make ritual offerings at the holy well. These were made up of Sarah's possessions: clothes, shoes, make up, shoulder bags, costume jewellery, hair brushes.

The group continued onwards, following the footpath up the field in the direction of St Martin's church. The drumming rhythm became more complex. Minor demons joined them: batlike and birdlike creatures that circled above the group, adding their eerie cries to the rhythm of the drums.

Sarah slipped and fell. She was dragged to her feet by Gareth and Rhys and stumbled on.

The group reached the churchyard gate and carried in the *Cailleach*. Olwen and the new Gatekeeper followed. Both groups filed into the church, with the *Cailleach* carried in first.

The pathway of silver moonlight that extended from the tumulus to the standing stone and on to St Martin's church filled the building with a pale wash of light. The drumming intensified, picking up pace.

A low mist, eerily white in the moonlight, began to creep from heather-clad hollows on Walden Moor and to gather along the courses of moorland streams.

In St Martin's church the lanterns were dimmed, the ancient stonework illuminated only by silver moonlight. The drumming changed to a spare and simple rhythm. Both groups, around forty persons, formed a half-circle in the nave, facing the tower arch expectantly.

The effigy was placed beneath the carved heads, as if it was about to address the assembly in the nave. The mouths of the heads glowed with a pale luminescence, as if filled with the light of the moon. A slow drum rhythm commenced.

Olwen released the Gatekeeper from the rope, forcing her to kneel on the floor of the nave. She pulled back the Gatekeeper's hood. The figure appeared to be in a heavily drugged trance.

Olwen pointed to the effigy. The drumming ceased.

"Awake!"

The *Cailleach* stirred and raised her arms. There was a long-drawn-out sigh from the assembly. Ectoplasm-like mist began to pour from the mouths of the three central heads: the Giant, Cernunnos and the Green Man...

In the churchyard sixty brown-robed monks, armed with knives, crossbows and lighted torches, surrounded the church. A black-cloaked figure and Reverend Dodds, both with torches, stood apart from them.

Reverend Dodds called out: "Watch and be ready! The Otherworld gateway is about to open!"

In the church Gwenda threw back her hood and drew a circle on the floor beneath the tower arch. The thickening ectoplasm flowed into the circle. Olwen removed the Gatekeeper's cloak, revealing her naked figure.

Olwen addressed her: "It is time for you to fulfil your function. To allow my forces to enter this world."

She pulled the Gatekeeper to her feet and pushed her into the circle. The Gatekeeper crouched in the circle, entwined by streamers of ectoplasm. Slowly she dematerialised.

"She is in place," Olwen announced. "Begin!"

Chapter Seventeen

A furious pounding drum rhythm thundered in the sacred space. The drumming and chanting had produced an altered state of consciousness in the assembled gathering and the group now experienced a hidden world of power that unleashed its terrifying reality within the walls of the old church.

A soul displacer, a spiral of shimmering multicoloured energy, materialised from the ectoplasm in the circle. It hovered for a moment, waves of colour radiating from it and swirling into the night sky. All at once it spun from the circle towards Olwen.

"Go!" she commanded. "Destroy our enemies!"

Soul displacers poured from St Martin's church. All that could be seen of them out in the churchyard was the spinning energy-spiral, hurtling between the gravestones with the unnerving speed of a desert djinn. Dodds's monks battled relentlessly. Some monks were too slow to react and promptly became possessed, turning and fighting their brethren with irresistible violence.

Reverend Dodds strode through the chaos, dispensing death at the point of his knife with the unerring efficiency of a battle-hardened veteran. He cut the throats of possessed monks, then reclaimed their souls with his cross. Any soul displacer within his long reach was incinerated with his flaming torch.

"Close up!" he ordered his fighters. "Don't let them through!"

The monks fought tirelessly. Many lay dead. The black-cloaked figure fought shoulder to shoulder with the survivors. Hesitant at first, he quickly found his fighting rhythm, cutting and burning his way across the churchyard, all the time working steadily towards the church doorway.

* * *

Out on the moor near the hilltop cairn two monks emerged from the cover of a stand of wind-blasted larches. One carried a heavy hammer, the other a long iron spike. They moved cautiously through knee-deep heather under the brilliant orb of the full moon, until they reached the pathway of silver light that extended across the moor.

One of the monks held the iron spike, while his companion drove it into the earth with blows from the hammer. No sooner had the spike been driven in than the pathway of silver light slowly began to fade.

At the same time, out by the tumulus on Walden Moor, two monks arose from a mist-filled hollow and made their way quickly on to the pathway of light. They were similarly equipped, one with a heavy hammer, the other with an iron spike. They began their work, but before they had delivered more than a half-dozen blows two terrifying Otherworld beings appeared on the tumulus:

One was a towering Shadow Man, his eyes and mouth filled with molten fire. By his side was a gigantic Black Dog, the creature's red eyes and muzzle licked by phosphorescent flame.

"Ancient guardians!" the first monk cried. "We have disturbed the World of the Dead!"

"Make haste!" his companion urged. "We must finish our task!"

The Shadow Man released the Black Dog, which galloped towards the monks along the pathway of light. The monks attempted to hammer in the spike but, with a stupendous howl, the Black Dog leaped upon them.

"Get back, foul creature!" the second monk yelled. "You have no power over the servants of God!"

He raised his cross to protect himself, but the Black Dog killed him with a blast of its toxic breath.

"Vile phantom, be gone!" screamed the first monk defiantly. "We are doing God's Work!"

He tried to drive in the spike by himself. He had almost succeeded when the Black Dog sprang on him. With a last desperate blow the monk hammered in the spike, as the Black Dog felled him with its breath, then threw back its head and filled the night with its triumphant blood-curdling howls.

But the pathway of light had been breached and it slowly began to fade. With a final chilling howl the Black Dog vanished into the tumulus. The Shadow Man lingered a few moments, then he too was gone.

* * *

In St Martin's churchyard battle raged between Dodds's monks and the soul displacers. Half the monks lay dead and new soul displacers kept coming. Reverend Dodds glanced towards the moors and saw that the pathway of light was fading.

"The energy field is broken! Fight harder!" he roared.

The black-cloaked figure had almost reached the church doorway but, before he could enter the church, two soul displacers burst through the doorway and rushed at him. He fought them off with knife and torch, but they persisted. If a third soul displacer had joined them the fight would have been over. But none came. A monk joined the fight by the church door and the two soul displacers were quickly destroyed with well aimed thrusts of his torch.

In the church a soul displacer began to materialise in the circle of ectoplasm, but it seemed unable to take form and collapsed to the floor with a sound like the shattering of crystal glass. The streamers of ectoplasm began slowly to withdraw into the mouths of the three carved heads.

"It's pulling back!" Rhiannon exclaimed.

"The energy field is failing!" Gareth realised.

"Dodds and his lackeys!" Olwen cried in fury.

The *Cailleach* suddenly lowered her arms.

There was a gasp of dismay from the assembly. The ectoplasm withdrew completely into the mouths of the heads on the tower arch.

Olwen turned to face the doorway as the black-cloaked figure strode in with his flaming torch. Paul threw back his hood.

"In the Name of God I denounce you!" he thundered. "In the Names of the Blessed Saints I denounce you! In the Name of the Holy Spirit I denounce you!"

The assembly surged forward, about to attack him. Their advance was halted abruptly as the thirty surviving monks, armed with lighted torches, crossbows and knives, entered the church.

"This place belongs to God!" Paul glared at Olwen. "I am here to reclaim it in His Name!"

"God? You invented him!" Olwen sneered.

"Your tricks and lies are as nothing to me!" Paul replied.

Olwen's manner appeared to soften. She morphed into her younger form. "I admire strong men like you. It's sad, seeing you waste your life here." She held her hands out towards him. "Come, be my consort. I can give you visions and adventure. I can give you true enlightenment. I can give you love."

Paul stepped away from her. "Only God is love," he stated adamantly.

"No gods can love, because they're not human," she countered.

"Return to the Otherworld where you belong!" he commanded.

She laughed. "Little priest, I could destroy you with the spit that's on my tongue! You cannot kill me. I embody the three great archetypes of the female principle. If you try to kill me I will change into a thousand life forms in as many seconds. You will never be fast enough to pin me down."

"We'll see who has the real power here!" He turned to the *Cailleach* that sat under the tower arch with no more presence now than a simple stuffed effigy. "I curse you, false idol, in the name of God's Holy Church!"

He applied his torch to the *Cailleach*.

With a horrific screech the effigy burst into flames and was consumed in a moment. With an agonised cry Olwen fell to the ground, where she morphed involuntarily into her menacing Crone archetype.

"Keep away from me, priest!" she cawed hoarsely. "Keep away!"

"I've come for my wife. You will release her!" he commanded.

"I will not!" She flung the words back at him like a curse.

He removed Reverend Dodds's cross from beneath his cloak.

"Release her!"

"Never!"

He pressed the cross to her forehead. "Yield, not to me, but to the minister of Christ!For His power presses upon thee, Who subdues thee beneath His Cross! Tremble at the power of His arm!"

Olwen, in her Crone archetype, hissed and writhed on the floor. Paul bent over her and pressed the cross even harder to her forehead.

"I command thee by the power of God and the Holy Ghost, that thou depart this place never to return! Give place to Christ who hath overcome thee."

With a terrible cry Olwen vanished.

In the next moment Sarah materialised on the floor. He went to her and wrapped her in his cloak.

"You will be safe now, my love," he said tenderly. "No more harm can ever come to you."

She did not respond. She seemed no more than an empty shell, a being without an animating soul. Before he could carry her from the church Reverend Dodds stepped from the shadows.

"Congratulations, Reverend Milton, you're a true warrior for God."

"You've no more to do with God than that sorceress!" Paul replied. "Religion's always been an excuse for war. All the pair of you want is power and control! And it will never be enough for you. You won't rest until you control the entire world!"

Dodds ignored Paul's outburst. "I required a man of God, who was pure in spirit and without fear."

"That rules you out, Dodds!" Paul replied with a savage laugh.

"I could not do battle with her," Reverend Dodds countered. "If I had defeated her I would have absorbed much of her power and become tempted to use it for personal gain. Not a situation I wish to experience! But your nature is proof against that – a rare disposition that cannot be corrupted by personal desire. Only you could defeat the sorceress and remain unharmed."

"You set us up!" Paul replied with bitter fury. "You knew from the very start that Sarah would be taken as the next Gatekeeper! You could have warned me! You put her life, her very soul, at risk!"

"Would you have done what you achieved this night if the odds had been less?" Dodds asked, fixing Paul with an icy stare.

Paul glared at him, this so-called Christian who showed not the slightest trace of human feeling.

When he banished Olwen he had passionately believed in what he was doing, as if he was the living spirit of his faith. Now he believed in nothing, except the urgent need to get Sarah the help she required.

"I must attend to my wife."

Without another word or a backward glance he picked Sarah up and carried her from the church.

Chapter Eighteen

Arthur was waiting by the churchyard gate and together they got Sarah back to the churchwarden's aging but practical Volvo Estate, which was parked at the T-junction in the Walden woods.

They placed Sarah gently on the back seat and covered her with Paul's cloak and a blanket Arthur had brought. As he was about to get into the passenger's seat Paul realised something had changed. He was unable to see much of the surrounding woodland in the moonlight, but he felt that the atmosphere was much less oppressive. The trees that he could make out, giant oaks and horse chestnuts, seemed not at all sinister or threatening. The influence from Walden had already begun to fade.

"Thanks for coming up, Arthur," Paul said. "I could never have managed otherwise. I no longer even have a car."

"I was concerned for you, up here alone and friendless," Arthur replied. "You wouldn't have had much support from Dodds."

"You're right there," Paul agreed. "There's no more humanity in him than a tree in the earth or a cloud in the sky."

He realised with a shock he was quoting Olwen Williams. How much of her world had he absorbed? Perhaps the influence from Walden was more pervasive than he thought…

As they drove back to Low Moor Arthur wondered what was happening back at St Martin's church.

"D'you think Dodds and his thugs will injure those pagan village folk up there, Paul? I mean, those monks are armed. They can do what they like with the locals."

"Dodds once told me he was a reclaimer of souls," Paul replied. "I imagine that's what he'll be trying to do. I think even he has seen enough violence for one night."

"Will there be peace? Could there even be a church congregation?"

Paul shook his head. "I don't have a crystal ball, Arthur. Neither do I want one! But I think it will take a formidable vicar to get anyone back to the church." He omitted to add that the vicar in question would not be himself.

* * *

In the spare bedroom in the churchwardens' cottage autumn sunlight flooded in through closed flower-patterned curtains. Sarah lay asleep in a single bed. She looked very pale. The dark flower shadows that played over the bed made her appear more pallid still. Paul and Beryl sat on opposite sides of the bed.

Paul held Sarah's hand. "I talked to her again this morning. And I noticed her hand seemed to have more warmth in it."

"That's a good sign, but she's still very fragile," Beryl said quietly. "Her soul was deeply damaged. It might take a long time for her to come through this."

He nodded in agreement, seeming resigned. "To be honest I wonder if she ever will. But I've made a bit of progress with my enquiries about specialist care."

Beryl seemed surprised. "I thought you'd no time for psychiatrists?"

"I haven't." He pulled a face. "Most of them are atheists. I have to go deeper. I have to find people with a tradition of specialist knowledge. We don't know enough about these matters in England today. But I think I might have made contact with people who do."

She shot him an enquiring glance, but he didn't elaborate.

"I'll let you know when I've found out a bit more." He smiled sadly. "For now all we can do is keep vigil and try to prevent her from slipping away from us. We must talk to her, even though she might not seem to hear us."

* * *

Paul joined Arthur in the vicarage garden while Beryl sat with Sarah. Arthur had got a fire going in an old metal school trunk left by a long-departed vicar. He had begun using it as an incinerator. Together they burned Olwen's paintings, both the ones from the vicarage and the one of Sarah as the Gatekeeper Paul had removed from Olwen's house. In the company of a half-dozen well armed monks they had taken the paintings of all the Gatekeepers away from Walden, to be locked in safe storage at Dodds's geomantic Institute.

"It's the best bonfire I've ever had," Arthur remarked, as the last of the paintings was consumed by the flames and the thin cries of the burning demons faded away.

"What will you do now?" Paul asked. "Will you stay to support the next vicar? I'm sure you've realised that it won't be me."

Arthur shook his head. "I'm only a few weeks from retirement. This war has taken more out of Beryl and me than we realised. We'll go back to our birth town, I think. We've a house there that's been rented out this past thirty years. My final act as churchwarden will be to give the record of past incumbents to the bishop." He hesitated, unsure if he should ask. "And you, Paul? D'you really think you've a future outside the church?"

"I have no doubts at all about that. I need to be free of all religious restrictions. I'll be staying with my parents in Oxford for a while, till something comes up." He felt it was inappropriate to say more. After all, his plans were far from finalised.

"Will Sarah be joining you when she's better?"

Poor Arthur, Paul thought. He couldn't face the fact that Sarah might never recover. But it would have been heartless to put those sentiments into words.

"That'll be up to Sarah. I'm not going to put her under any pressure. She's endured far too much already."

As the fire died down Paul left Arthur to rake through the last smouldering fragments. He had a lot on his mind, none of which he could speak of until he got to Oxford.

He was already aware that the decisions he made from now on would only affect himself. He was in the process of preparing to remove Sarah to the best place he could find for her. It was a sanatorium in the Italian mountains run by Catholic nuns from an order specialising in the treatment of spiritual trauma, everything from psychic attacks to cases of violent possession. He had not spoken with them about Gatekeepers or soul displacers, saying simply that his wife had been the victim of multiple states of diabolical possession.

Since he had become aware of James West's geomantic plan and the revelatory contents of Dodds's cabinet a growing sense of urgency had taken hold of him. He realised that a long conversation with certain of his parents' intellectual friends was imperative.

What the outcome of this would be he had no idea. But the conversation had to come first and then, possibly, a course of action. But he knew with absolute certainty that a country in the hands of a Julius Dodds or an Olwen Williams was not a good place to be. It was bad enough already, with concerns about national security eroding personal freedoms, not to mention the rise of nationalism throughout Europe.

He borrowed Arthur's Volvo and drove out to Walden for what he hoped would be the last time. To his intense annoyance he met Reverend Dodds at the gate to St Martin's churchyard. Four armed monks accompanied him.

"Good day to you, Paul," Dodds intoned. "The air up here is much sweeter than it used to be, don't you think?"

"Are you still hunting soul displacers, Julius?" Paul asked. "Were there many that escaped us?"

"We've come to the end of them at last, I think. I'm just making sure there are none skulking around up here, looking for a way to return to the Otherworld."

Paul was half way down the churchyard path when he heard Dodds addressing him again.

"I'm thinking of holding open-air services up here in the spring, once the place has been thoroughly exorcised. I might bring in worshippers from outside the area. The novelty of it might attract them." Receiving no response from Paul, he added: "I'll be moving on to other potential gateways later next year. I wondered if I might send for you if I have problems?"

Paul turned and gave him a withering look. "I have only one wife, Julius. My responsibility to Sarah comes first. I thought you might have realised that. Anyway, by Christmas I won't even be a vicar. You'll be getting my letter of resignation in the next few days."

"You don't have to be an officer of the Christian church to fight demons," Dodds replied. "You have just to be the man you already are."

"I'll have to think about it," Paul replied. "But that's a long way from being a 'yes'."

* * *

He stood for a while looking up at the carved heads on the tower arch. It was almost impossible to believe that they had been the focus of such dark and arcane rites as he had witnessed.

Was this the final confrontation, he wondered? Or was it merely a dress rehearsal for many such future 'wars'? Would the struggle for spiritual and temporal control ever end?

He realised Julius Dodds had the opportunity to remove the heads and wondered if he would do so. Without the sorceress and a supportive pagan community the heads had no power or purpose. He was surprised Dodds's monks hadn't already smashed them to dust.

He wondered if Dodds wanted to use the gateway himself in order to enhance his personal power. But he dismissed the notion as absurd. Surely the man wouldn't be tempted to be so insanely reckless...

The heads on that late-autumn afternoon looked faintly sinister, but their potential as Otherworld portals was hidden from those who possessed no arcane knowledge. They were mere archaic curiosities, attracting the likes of Joan Preston to ponder the rich strangeness of former pagan times.

Yes, he thought as he turned to go, there's much to discuss with my parents' circle. He just hoped he would be talking to receptive minds. He could speak with authority because he had lived through the situations he was going to present to them...

Unnoticed by Paul, in the pattern of lichen on the nave wall, the tripartite simulacrum of Olwen Williams seemed for a moment to stir, as if watching him leave.

Dear reader,

We hope you enjoyed reading *The Gatekeeper.* Please take a moment to leave a review, even if it's a short one. Your opinion is important to us.

Discover more books by Ian Taylor at
https://www.nextchapter.pub/authors/ian-taylor

Want to know when one of our books is free or discounted? Join the newsletter at http://eepurl.com/bqqB3H

Best regards,
Ian Taylor, Rosi Taylor and the Next Chapter Team

You might also like:
Catching Phantoms by Ian Taylor and Rosi Taylor

To read the first chapter for free, please head to:
https://www.nextchapter.pub/books/catching-phantoms

The Gatekeeper
ISBN: 978-4-86751-612-6

Published by
Next Chapter
1-60-20 Minami-Otsuka
170-0005 Toshima-Ku, Tokyo
+818035793528
5th July 2021